# THE NATCHEZ TRACE

The history of the Natchez Trace is one of bloody feuds, of sudden and violent death, and of the men who made the West. Men such as Aaron Lewis, the young lawyer who fought the powerful, evil syndicates trying to move in and take over the land granted to the settlers by the government in Washington. Then there was Dan Carson, gunfighter and gambler. For these two conflicting characters, personal emotions are magnified many times by danger and violence.

ALAN ROBERTS

# THE NATCHEZ TRACE

*Complete and Unabridged*

## LINFORD
*Leicester*

First hardcover edition published in Great Britain
in 2002 by Robert Hale Limited, London

Originally published in paperback as
*The Landbreakers* by Chuck Adams

First Linford Edition
published 2004
by arrangement with
Robert Hale Limited, London

The moral right of the author has been asserted

Copyright © 2002 by John Glasby
All rights reserved

British Library CIP Data

Roberts, Alan, 1928–
 The Natchez trace.—Large print ed.—
Linford western library
1. Western stories
2. Large type books
I. Title II. Adams, Chuck. Landbreakers
823.9'14 [F]

ISBN 1–84395–202–5

Published by
F. A. Thorpe (Publishing)
Anstey, Leicestershire

Set by Words & Graphics Ltd.
Anstey, Leicestershire
Printed and bound in Great Britain by
T. J. International Ltd., Padstow, Cornwall

This book is printed on acid-free paper

# 1

## Each Man His Own Law

In the beginning, as he went about his usual evening ritual of setting up the type on the press, checking over the various items for the next day's edition, he kept his waning courage alive by telling himself that he was the only person in New Orleans who was in a position to tell the ordinary townsfolk the truth of what was happening about them, that he had told Tollinson that he had a sacred duty to print what he knew to be true and that nothing would be allowed to stop him. The idea, he told himself, was to allow his thoughts to go no further than that. He knew that Tollinson didn't like some of the articles he had published and the other had threatened, on several occasions, that he would be forced to do something about it if he didn't stop printing these stories of the big syndicates that were working, both here in New Orleans, and all the way back along the Natchez Trace, to deprive the settlers of the land which had been granted them by the Government.

He knew that Tollinson had been bringing men in over the past few days, rough men, professional gunfighters who followed no law but their own and would do whatever Tollinson asked them to do. He was not so much afraid for himself as for his daughter Jennifer. What would they do to her if he did not stop printing this news? He laid a new line of type into place, finding in this simple act a feeling of strength and fresh courage, but there was sweat on his forehead and on the palms of his hands and a handful of type fell from his fingers and scattered on the floor.

Forcing breath into his lungs, he bent to pick it up, fingers still shaking a little. When the outer door opened with a sharp click, he jerked himself unsteadily to his feet, rubbing the sweat from his forehead before it could run into his eyes.

'Evening, Nathan.' Aaron Lewis came in, closed the street door behind him. 'Just thought I'd drop in and see how things were going.' He seated himself on the corner of the nearby table, one leg swinging idly.

Nathan had jumped at the other's voice and he knew now just how much of his earlier courage had been more than pure bravado, but the last few days had been drawing in on his last small reserves of courage. He shrugged and made a great show of his casualness.

'Couldn't be better,' he said harshly. He placed the type he had picked up from the floor back into the box at his side, locked that which he had already set into place and carried it over to the press.

'Any more trouble with Tollinson? I heard he'd threatened to smash up your place and run you out of town if you didn't stop printing those articles about him.'

'He did come to see me, but I soon put him right on that,' said the other thinly. 'I publish the New Orleans Courier and I mean to see that everybody in town knows what's happening right here under their noses.'

'Do you think it will make the slightest difference to them?' asked the lawyer frankly. 'I've talked to some of these settlers who've been run off their land, tried to do something for them, but if they won't stand together, then there's nothing we can do.'

'Then you think we ought to let this go on?' Nathan shook his heavy head. 'I think far too much of the truth to allow that to happen, while I still have the means to fight it, Aaron.'

'I know how you feel, Nathan. But you're only one man and these killers mean every word they say. They'll stop at nothing to stop you and believe me, nobody in this town will lift a finger to help you if Tollinson makes a move.'

'Then the Government will have to do something to stop it.'

'The Government!' Lewis got to his feet, a tall, darkly handsome man, features lean and tanned. His tone held a tight ring of sarcasm. 'They're too far away in Washington to worry about what goes on here. This is a problem which will have to be solved here and by us; but at the moment, we have no way of backing up any move we make.'

'But this is the first move,' said Nathan desperately. 'Some day the settlers will band together and fight for their rights. Until then, we have to do it for them.'

Across the distance, from the direction of the levee, there drifted the dull, moaning wail of a steamboat. Nathan's skin felt prickly again at the sound, although he did not know why it should affect him in this way.

Clamping the type into place, he started the press and for a long moment there was no sound in the room apart from the clattering of the machinery.

Tiredness rode in Nathan's body and the muscles of his chest and stomach churned a little from reaction. He found himself glancing alertly at the window whenever anyone went by on the boardwalk, feeling a little tingle run through him whenever anyone paused outside the office. The lawyer's presence there should have given him some comfort, but it didn't.

'You're jumpy, Nathan. Maybe you'd better let this thing ride for a day or two, just put out the usual articles. Give Tollinson a chance to simmer down a little. You know that he's been bringing men in on the steamers.'

'I know,' said the other shortly. He sighed. 'Why is it that in every age we have to have men like Tollinson and the others?'

Aaron smiled faintly. 'It's a sign of progress. Whenever the pioneers have moved in and established a frontier, the crooked gamblers and the gunfighters move in at their back and there's inevitably a period of violence until law and order prevail.' He moved over to the door, paused and glanced back at the other. 'I'd think things over very carefully, Nathan, before you do anything you may regret. I wouldn't like there to be any trouble.'

Nathan shook his head. He nodded towards the heavy gun leaning against the wall nearby. 'I reckon I can take care of myself, Aaron,' he said softly. 'But thanks for the concern.'

He listened to the other walk away, footsteps fading on the creaking boardwalk outside the building. Then he turned back to his work. He was already behind schedule with the printing and for almost an hour, he became absorbed in his work. As he worked, a sickness grew in him, a sickness that came from the knowledge that Aaron had been right, that there was no way yet of fighting these men. Even the Courier, read as it was by most of the townsfolk in New Orleans, could not make them sit up and take notice of what was happening around them. He was wishing now, too late, that he might have done something more to bring to the attention of these people the evil that lived and moved among them. He had printed everything he had been able to discover about the other, had published the facts about the title deeds for the stretches of land along both sides of the Natchez Trace which had somehow found their way into Tollinson's possession.

He could have got himself a gun and gone out to turn his words into action, but when he had looked over the other, he had known that these were just wild imaginings of his mind and that he would never be able to kill the other, no matter how evil he knew him to be. But Aaron Lewis's words had cemented his decision. If the young lawyer could do nothing, then it was up to him.

He did not hear the street door open. He only felt the gust of cold air that swirled around him as he bent over the press. Nathan felt his stomach tighten as he straightened up and turned.

Tollinson grinned at him viciously as he closed the outer door gently behind him. He said sharply: 'I wouldn't go for that rifle if I were you, because you'll be dead before you can reach it if you try.' He jerked a thumb in the direction of the window and Nathan saw the two men who stood outside, peering into the office, their hands hovering close to the butts of the guns in their belts.

'That's better,' said Tollinson as the other forced himself to relax. He walked over and picked up one of the printed sheets, moved across to where the lamp rested on the long, low table, and held the paper out so that he could read it. His face did not change as he glanced through the items on the front page. Then he deliberately tore up the sheet into small pieces and dropped them on to the floor in front of him.

'Seems to me that you won't listen when you're given very good advice,' said the other in that same soft voice. He came forward again, not once taking his glance from the other's face. 'You have proved to be rebellious on too many occasions and I've no alternative now but to see that the lesson you learn will be a lasting one.' He walked over to the door, opened it and called: 'Will, Ben. Come here. There's work for you to do.'

As the two men outside the office moved, Nathan dived sideways for the rifle, leaning against the wall. His fingers had closed about it, and he was turned half towards the door when the blast of fire sounded loud in the room and he fell back with the bullet in his shoulder, the gun dropping from nerveless fingers as he staggered, clutched at his shoulder, looking down with a look of dismayed amazement at the blood that dribbled slowly between his fingers, soaking into his shirt.

'That slug could have gone through your heart,' chided Tollinson. He gestured the two men into the room, closed and locked the door, and then pulled down the shutters over the windows. 'We don't want any interruptions with our business this time,' he said, his voice soft and seemingly remote, but with a trace of menace in it that did not pass unnoticed as far as Nathan was concerned.

Coming back into the middle of the room, Tollinson stood for a moment, staring about him. A thin smile touched his lips, twisting them into a cruel gash across his features. 'Seems a pity to have to destroy all of this,' he said harshly. 'You really should have heeded my warning, you know.'

Sensing what the other intended to do, Nathan moved forward, ignoring the pain that washed through his shoulder as he moved. A cry built up in his throat and he cried out thinly: 'You touch any of this, Tollinson, and by God I'll see that you regret it. I swear I'll — '

Tollinson swung on him sharply. 'You'll be in no position to do anything,' he rasped, 'You've troubled me for the last time. I said I'd have to stop you permanently, and I mean to do so.'

He gave a quick signal with his right hand, gesturing towards the press. Grinning viciously, the two gunhawks moved towards it, grasped it tightly on either side and heaved it over with grunts of strain. The heavy piece of machinery tilted precariously, then crashed forward on to its side, pieces of type spilling all over the floor. Nathan started forward, face twisting. His eyes were starting from his head as he saw all of his precious equipment being smashed in front of him, but Tollinson whipped a small gun from his belt and levelled it on the other's stomach, his eyes glittering brightly in his head.

'Just stay back there,' he warned thickly, 'otherwise I'll have to shoot you down before you've seen what happens to people who stand in my way.'

Nathan stood away from the other, feeling the blood oozing down from his torn shoulder, the dull ache suffusing through his whole body. He was forced to stand there and watch while the men systematically smashed up every piece of machinery in the room, tipping the boxes of type on to the floor, grinding them into unrecognizable pieces of metal with their heels.

This was what Aaron Lewis had warned him about, he thought dully, men who stopped at nothing to gain their own evil ends. Anger stormed through him, making him heedless and reckless and he rushed at Tollinson, hoping to get his arms around the other before he could pull the trigger of that gun in his hand.

The sudden manoeuvre took the other by surprise. He had clearly not expected Nathan to make any move. Savagely, Nathan lashed out with his fist, felt a sense of satisfaction as his knuckles jolted solidly against the other's face, grazing along his cheek. A savage joy leapt in him as he struck again, sending Tollinson reeling back against the overturned press. Blood spurted from Tollinson's lips as the blow took him full on the mouth. He gave a strangled yell of anger and pain, tried to squirm away, the gun slipping from his fingers, clattering on to the floor. Nathan kicked at it with his boot, sent it sliding into the far corner of the room.

He aimed another wild swing at the man in front of him, missed as the other managed to roll away. His momentum carried him forward, off-balance, and at the same moment, one of the gunmen, moving forward at Tollinson's cry, brought the butt of his gun crashing down on the back of his head, pitching him forward on to the floor.

Breathing heavily, Tollinson drew himself upright, sucking air down into his lungs, rubbing the back of his hand over his bleeding mouth. 'Get some oil,' he snarled viciously, 'and we'll finish this job properly.'

'What about him?' asked one of the men.

'No need to worry about him,' said

Tollinson. He aimed a kick at the inert body on the floor at his feet. His eyes were wild and anger still suffused his face. He had lost his hat in the struggle and his hair hung down in front of his eyes.

One of the men rummaged around in the corner of the room, came back a moment later with a can of oil.

'Spread it over everything,' Tollinson ordered. 'When we've finished, there'll be no more New Orleans Courier.' He managed a grin in spite of his bloodied mouth. He watched as the other sprinkled the oil over the smashed machinery, on to the floor and the papers which had been strewn everywhere. Soon, the whole place reeked of it and Tollinson gave a satisfied nod. He picked up the lamp from the desk, carried it carefully back with him to the street door.

'Let's get out of here,' he said harshly. He waited until the two men had moved out into the quiet, dark street, paused for a moment in the

15

doorway, then tossed the lamp into the room and ran back as a sheet of flame swept over the oil-covered floor. Within seconds, the whole of the outer office was a raging inferno. Tollinson felt the blast of heat wash over him, felt his skin draw tight on his bones. Then he slipped back into the shadows, running on the heels of the two gunmen. They moved swiftly along the narrow alley that ran beside the office, moving in silence until they reached the end of the alley, where three horses stood waiting for them. Saddling up, they rode swiftly out into the night.

* * *

Aaron Lewis stood in the wide, dusty street and watched the smoking ruins of the Courier office. The flames were dying down now and he walked forward slowly, turned abruptly as he saw the figure of the girl standing beside the wall. He said sharply: 'Jennifer! What happened here?'

The girl turned her head slowly. For a moment it was as if she had not heard, almost as if she did not even recognize him. Her glance was stone-still, her lips half-parted. Her voice shook a little as she answered: 'My father's dead, Aaron.'

He stepped beside her, watched the way her mouth struggled to keep from loosening. Her eyes screwed themselves up. She wanted to cry again, but did not want any one to see it. He put his arms around her, drew her to him, felt her head go down on to his shoulder and her body begin to shake as she cried again, the tears which trickled down her cheeks, falling warm and wet on the back of his hand.

One of the men standing nearby, said: 'I've had a word with the marshal, but there doesn't seem much he can do at the moment. Nobody seems to have seen anything. Could have been an accident. He was evidently working here getting the paper ready for tomorrow and he may have upset the lamp on the desk.'

The girl shook her head. Holding her, Aaron felt the misery that was in her, struggling to get out. He struggled to put his riotous thoughts into some kind of order in his mind, knowing that whatever it was that had happened here, in the few minutes since he had left Nathan, it had not been an accident. The office would not have burned like that unless somebody had carefully poured oil on to the floor and outlined against the flames, he could just see the huge bulk of the press where it had been pushed over on to its side. It would have taken at least two strong men to move a weight such as that. Certainly Nathan could not have done it unaided, even if he had intended to.

He said quietly, to the girl: 'I'll take you over to the hotel, Jennifer. You won't have any place to stay now. When you've had a night's sleep, we'll talk this over.'

'Talk!' There was a sudden sharp

fierceness in her voice which astonished him. She pulled herself out of his arms, checked her crying, wiped her eyes. He saw her put this tragedy away from her for a moment, saw her tighten her self-control and discipline her mind with a tremendous effort. 'Nobody seems to do anything around here but talk. My father was the only man who had the courage to do anything more and now he's dead. Everybody knows it was Tollinson who murdered him. Why try to hide it and call it an accident?'

'Now we don't know that Tollinson did have anything to do with this, Jennifer,' Aaron said slowly, choosing his words carefully, knowing how the girl felt. In his own mind, he had the feeling that what she said was probably true. After all, he had warned Nathan about printing these articles about Tollinson only a little while before he had died. But thinking that Tollinson was the killer, and proving it were two different things; and even if they did succeed in proving it, there was little they could do about it. Tollinson was far too powerful a man for the law to touch.

The girl spoke through the short, quick lifts of her breath. 'You know it was Tollinson. He's been saying he'll kill my father ever since those articles were printed.'

Aaron took her gently by the arm and led her away from the scene, across the street and over to the hotel. 'I'll get you a room for the night, Jennifer,' he said quietly, but firmly. 'Like I said, we'll talk this over in the morning. In the meantime, try to get some sleep.'

She shook her head slowly. 'I won't be able to sleep tonight.' She showed him an expression that meant nothing to him, her features tight with pain and worry. 'My father tried to play a game he wasn't meant to play, and because of it, because he tried to show the ordinary people of this town where their duty lay, he was killed.'

'I tried to warn him earlier this evening, told him what might happen if he persisted in this idea of his, but he wouldn't listen to me.'

'You warned him?' She looked at him in sudden surprise. 'You saw my father tonight?'

'That's right. I dropped in to see him about two hours ago. He was just setting up everything. I told him to take things easy for a while as far as Tollinson is concerned. To leave these things up to the law, wait until the Government got to hear about what's happening and then — '

'That's what everybody wanted, wasn't it? For him to stop printing these things about Tollinson. Nobody seemed to care what happened to those people who were driven from their homes, who lost all of their land, or who were shot down because they refused to sell out to Tollinson.'

Aaron avoided answering the implied question by changing the subject. 'I'll talk with you in the morning, Jennifer. In the meantime, try to get some rest, even if you aren't able to sleep.'

21

He turned on his heel and walked back into the street. The small crowd in front of the burnt-out offices was beginning to disperse now. Marshal Thorpe gave Aaron a sideways glance as the lawyer stepped up on to the boardwalk beside him.

'This is a bad business, Aaron,' he said shortly. 'A bad business indeed.'

'You got any idea who did it?' asked the other pointedly.

Thorpe shook his head heavily. 'Might have been an accident,' he said softly.

'Now you don't really mean that, Marshal.' Aaron eyed the other sharply, giving him a bright stare. 'You saw that press. It would have taken two men to have pushed that over on to its side, two men stronger than Nathan King and there must have been paraffin all over that room for it to have blazed up as it did.'

'Very likely you're right,' said the other musingly. He struck a match on the wall, applied it to the end of his cheroot. The tip glowed redly as he drew deeply on it. 'You think his daughter realizes that?'

'I'm sure she does.'

'What do you think she'll do about this?' There was an edge of worry to the marshal's tone.

'I'm not sure.' Aaron rubbed his chin thoughtfully. 'If I knew that I might feel a lot easier in my mind. I'm not certain but that she might not decide to stay here and carry on with what Nathan was trying to do.'

'And you're afraid that if she does that, Tollinson may try to kill her too.'

'He'll try,' said Aaron. 'I'm just wondering which way he'll try.'

Thorpe shrugged his shoulders, stared down at the glowing tip of the cheroot for a long moment. 'I want to keep this town peaceable. But somehow I've got the feeling I'm sitting on top of a powder keg and Nathan, even though he's dead, has just lit the fuse. This whole town, clear along the Trace as well, is going to erupt if things get out of hand.' His voice revealed some strain and some emphasis.

Aaron took the news with his usual grave and calm manner. 'That's what I figured,' he nodded. 'Whatever happens, I feel we have to talk Jennifer out of trying to carry on with her father's work. The trouble is, she's a strong-willed girl, and she may not take any heed of what we tell her.'

$$\star \quad \star \quad \star$$

One bright wave of sunlight broke over the hills, which at this point, crowded close to the banks of the Mississippi, shattering the dimness of the dawn, the suddenness with which it had appeared like a great washing of water over the countryside. The trees which stood on the upper slopes of the hills changed their hue from a dark grey to green within seconds as the light touched them.

Standing at the rail of the steamer, Dan Carson let his gaze drift over the scenery which moved slowly past him. At this time of the morning, the air was clear and cool and the strike of the steamer's bow in the swirling water ran the spreading ripples clear to either bank, the wash running back along the shore almost as far as the eye could see. The Big Muddy was still well up with the melting of the winter snows high in the distant mountains and they were making good time on their way down to New Orleans.

Soon, they would be leaving the small towns along this stretch of the river behind and entering the wilderness and then the southern reaches of the vast river. They turned a wide, sweeping bend just as the sun lifted over the crests of the hills and the river sparkled like a shining highway on which the steamer moved slowly, ponderously almost, engines throbbing mightily, paddles churning the water into a white streaming of foam, with the thin clanging of the signal bells touching the rising banks and being thrown back at them as fainter echoes.

Lifting his head, he squinted up at the sun, eyes narrowed. He was a tall man, narrow-hipped, with a rider's looseness about him, a man a little uneasy on water. The sun had placed a deep tan on his features and as he looked directly at the sun, grey eyes half hidden behind the low drop of his lids, he turned his inward attention on some of his fellow passengers. Most of them were the usual run of people who travelled the length of this great river. Merchants and a sprinkling of gamblers, a few men in uniform travelling to take up a post somewhere along the frontier. But there were three others whose type he had recognized at once. Squat men, faces angular, wearing their guns low on their hips, men who sold their guns to the highest bidder, possibly keeping one jump ahead of the law. He fell to wondering why they were on this boat, knew they meant trouble for somebody. The most likely thing was that they were headed for New

Orleans, where there were plenty of opportunities for men of this breed to join one of the bands who rode the Natchez Trace, preying on the whipsawers. He had heard something of the way these gangs operated. Once the steamboats reached New Orleans and the rivermen were paid off, they were forced to head back to Kentucky overland along the Natchez Trace and it was along this trail that most of the rich pickings were to be had. Outlaws could often corner a man with gold in his saddlebags along an empty stretch of the trail.

After breakfast, he remained in his cabin for the rest of the morning. He had been fortunate in being able to get a first-class berth on the boat and the cabin was more comfortable than he had expected. When he finally returned to the deck, several of the passengers were lining the rails as they churned their way through thickly-wooded country, the trees growing right down to the banks. There were still several more days on the river before they reached New Orleans and whenever they wooded, the mate and a handful of the crew would go ashore with rifles and shoot game, or bring the wood back on board to feed the mighty boilers of the boat.

He found himself a vacant place at the rail, leaned forward and peered down into the swirling brown, muddy waters that flowed past the side of the boat.

The heat of the afternoon lay heavy on his back and shoulders and he scarcely noticed the man who came foreward and stood beside him, resting his ponderous weight on his elbows, pausing now and again to mop his forehead with a large red handkerchief.

'This your first trip down river to New Orleans?' asked the other.

Dan turned, found himself staring into a round, florid face on which a film of sweat glistened slightly in the glaring sunlight. He nodded slowly. 'How did you guess?'

'That wasn't too difficult,' boomed the other loudly. He smiled broadly. 'You don't seem the usual kind of man one finds on these steamers. You'd look more at home in the saddle — or am I wrong?' His eyes were shrewd as he gave Dan a bright-sharp stare.

'You're right.' Dan rolled himself a smoke, turning and leaning his back against the rail. Judging from the other's tight-fitting frock-coat and silk waistcoat, the other was either a merchant or a gambler, it was difficult to tell which at this first acquaintance.

'I thought so. Permit me to introduce myself. Andrew Tollinson. I own a cattle ranch a few miles west of New Orleans.'

The other nodded. 'My name is Carson, Dan Carson. I guess you'd say I'm just a drifter.'

'Even a drifter can find a useful place in this country if he's willing to accept things as they are and he isn't too particular about the kind of work he does,' said the other enigmatically.

'Just what does that mean?' Dan

asked. He lit the cigarette, sucked smoke down into his lungs, then let it out again slowly through his nostrils. 'You offering me a job?'

'Perhaps. I could always use a good man.' The other's eyes grew speculative. 'You need to understand how things are on the frontier, Mr Carson. There are powerful forces at work there, many of them trying to stifle the growth of this country. Unfortunately, they masquerade under the guise of people anxious to do good. One has to be hard if this new country is to be tamed. Softness is a good thing but there are ways here which too many people do not understand.'

'But why are you telling me this?'

Tollinson ran his hard gaze over the other for a second before replying.

'Because you look to me like a man who can handle a gun and who isn't afraid to use it.'

'And you need somebody who can kill a man without asking too many questions. Is that it, Mr Tollinson?'

'That's a hard way of putting it,' acknowledged the other. He looked a trifle uncomfortable, as if he could not quite size up this man, almost as if he now knew that he had said a little more than he had intended without getting to know this man a little more. He appeared to deliberate for a moment, trying to find words for what was in his mind. 'You don't belong to these parts?'

'I don't,' Dan admitted. His face was still hard.

'You going to New Orleans on business or just for pleasure?'

'Perhaps a little of both.' Dan was deliberately noncommittal. He dragged smoke into his lungs. 'But you were talking about hiring a man who would kill and ask no questions.'

'Well, yes I was.' The other studied Dan's face closely. 'Like I said, this is wild country, not yet tamed, and a man has to take certain precautions to safeguard his own. There are several men who would like to take away what I've got, men who would stop at nothing to rustle my cattle, take away my land, even lie to make it seem that I'm in the wrong.'

'Do those other three *hombres* on board work for you?' Dan asked pointedly.

The other lifted his thick, bushy brows a little. 'I have three of my men with me,' he said after a pause. 'Now don't get me wrong. I don't aim to involve you in my troubles if you figure this isn't the kind of work for you.'

'Seems to me that what you're aiming to do is take over as much of the territory around New Orleans as you can and anybody who stands in your way will either be shot or run out of the state.' Dan spoke calmly and coolly, but he felt a sharp anger rising in his mind.

Tollinson swung about. A sudden gleam came to his eyes, then they clouded. 'Now see here, Mr Carson. You don't look like a man who pushes himself in where he's not wanted, but if you should start getting any ideas at all about — '

'Now you're not trying to threaten me are you, Mr Tollinson?' Dan's lips thinned into a tight line. 'I don't take kindly to threats.'

Tollinson stared at him. There seemed to be an answer to that balanced in his mind but he took several seconds before speaking. 'Like you've already figured, I've got three of my men on board with me. They'll be staying until we get off at New Orleans. I don't want any trouble on the voyage, I always detest violence if it can be possibly avoided. But I'd advise you to think over my offer. The pay is good and if you should be running one jump ahead of the law, there'd be no need to worry further on that score.' Eyes narrowed a little, he swung about and moved away from the rail. Dan watched him as he moved along the deck, then paused to talk earnestly with the three men near the stern. Out of the corner of his eye, Dan saw the men glance in his direction, then look away again. Evidently, he thought with a sudden tightening of the muscles of his chest, the other was warning them of what had happened. There was no knowing to what lengths Tollinson might go to prevent a stranger from butting into his business, even though the other had been the one to broach the subject of working for him.

\* \* \*

He could have been sleeping for hours, or it might have been only a few minutes, but something brought Dan awake and he sat up in the narrow bunk, straining his ears to pick out the sound that had cut down through this consciousness and wakened him, touching that part of his mind which never slept. Outside the cabin he could hear the faint slap of the water against the side of the boat and the engines were still throbbing, although the sound was muffled here. There seemed to be no other sound, nothing out of place that could explain what had disturbed him.

Maybe it had been only a dream, he told himself after a few moments. He contemplated lying back on the bunk and going to sleep, but acting on impulse, he swung his legs to the floor and got to his feet, feeling the faint roll and sway of the boat under him. The air was warm inside the small cabin and he reached out for his trousers, pulling them on quickly, then buckled on the heavy gunbelt. He felt a sudden desire for a smoke, reached into the pocket of his jacket, hanging over the chair beside the bunk, then changed his mind, straightening up. Again came that sound which had awakened him, the soft sound of someone moving around on the deck, almost outside the door of his cabin.

Silently, he padded forward, gently twisted the key in the lock and turned the handle slowly, pulling the door open. The faint creak of the hinges was lost in the clanking of the paddlewheel. Cautiously, he peered out, glancing along the deck in both directions. He was fully alert now, feeling danger all about him, but not certain from which direction it would come.

Since that day, some ten days earlier, when he had had that conversation with Andrew Tollinson, he had experienced the uneasy feeling that the other had regretted telling him as much as he had, and did not intend that he should reach New Orleans alive, possibly recognizing that he could harm him if he should get there and start asking questions around the townsfolk.

The moon was up now, throwing yellow light along the river, bathing the boat in brilliance. Although he could see along the stretch of deck alongside his cabin, and noticed that it was empty, there were too many moon-thrown shadows about in which a would-be attacker might hide. He stood there for a long moment, waiting for the faint sound to be repeated so that he might know in which direction the man was.

Then his keen gaze picked out the

shadow of a man standing behind one of the heavy beams less than ten yards away. Dan's eyes narrowed. Slowly, he eased his way out of the cabin, moved across the deck to the rail and edged around the deck so as to come up behind the other. Now he could just make out the shape of the man, knew it was one of the three killers that Tollinson had hired. Grimly, he moved closer, the revolver held tightly in his right hand. Coming up behind the unsuspecting man, he said thinly: 'Don't make any wrong moves or try to go for your gun, or I'll kill you.'

He felt the man stiffen, move his hand away from his gun with an obvious reluctance.

'That's better. Now maybe you'll tell me what you're doing here.'

'Can't a man take a walk on deck without having a gun pushed into his back?' grunted the other harshly. 'What is this, a hold-up?'

'You know damned well it isn't,' Dan snapped. 'I suppose that Tollinson told you to kill me and drop my body over the side into the Mississippi.'

'I don't know what you're talking about,' said the other thickly.

'But you don't deny that you've been hired by Tollinson.'

'No. Why should I deny it?' The other half-turned his head, as if trying to make out who he was, to confirm his own suspicions. The other was clearly trying to figure out how Dan had managed to get there at his back and take him by surprise in this way, obviously cursing himself for not having kept a closer eye on the door of the cabin.

'I figured that would be the way of it.' Dan thrust the barrel of the gun harder into the other's back, heard the man's sharp intake of air as he gasped with agony. 'Where are those other two *hombres* that Tollinson hired? Or were you the only one ordered to kill me?'

'You're talking in riddles,' grunted the other. 'Now take that gun out of my back before I yell for the Captain. I'm just a passenger on this ship and — '

Too late, Dan realized that the other had been talking to gain time, that he had not been alone there. He half-heard the soft tread behind him, turned his head to meet this new menace which had suddenly presented itself, twisting his body instinctively to one side like a cat. The blow which had been aimed at the back of his skull and which would probably have killed him had it connected, struck him on the shoulder, momentarily numbing his arm, the gun dropping from nerveless fingers which no longer seemed to have any feeling in them.

Swiftly, he whirled on his heels, saw the grinning, bearded face of one of the other men behind him, right arm upraised to swing downward again with the reversed gun. There was little time in which to think and less in which to act. Dan saved his life by ducking swiftly under the blow, doubling his left fist and sending a sharp punch into the other's belly. The blow drove the wind out of the other, sent him staggering back, hands dropping, fingers spread fanwise across his agony-filled stomach. His mouth had sprung wide open and he stood there in obvious pain, without breath in his body and momentarily unable to get it.

By now, the other man had recovered, was already coming at Dan, arms flailing wildly. One swing caught Dan on the side of the face and he felt the shock of it jar through his cheek and down the muscles of his neck into his body. Another blow roared through Dan's brain and the moonlight dimmed in front of him. He fell back under the other's furious onslaught. The feeling was coming back into his shoulder and arm only gradually and with only one good hand, he doubted if he had the ability to fight off these two men, and God alone knew where the third man was, possibly waiting somewhere in the shadows until these two had worn him down sufficiently. Then the other would step in and end the fight.

The man at his back threw his arms around him from behind, tried to haul him off his feet, but Dan swung him about with a savage strength, forcing him to release his hold, sending him sprawling across the deck where he finished up against the rails, cracking his skull on them with a sickening force. He lay on his back with his eyes closed, unmoving.

Turning to face the first man, Dan felt his senses leaving him, sure that if he lost consciousness he was done for. He would be dropped over the side of the boat and the packet would steam on, the rest of the crew and passengers not knowing what had happened to him, uncaring perhaps. There were often dangerous elements on a ship like this and the less notice one took of these happenings, the safer, the healthier one would be. As the man tried to hit him again, he lashed out with his boot, caught his attacker behind the knees and sent him pitching forward. As the man went down with a faint gasp of agony, he caught Dan around the knees and brought him down on to the hard deck. Dan hit hard on his shoulder blades. As he twisted round to face the other, he saw the man heaving himself back on to his haunches. For some reason the other had released his hold just when he had the upper hand. Then Dan saw why. The moonlight which flooded over the deck glittered bluely on the blade in the other's hand as the man set himself to throw. He was obviously not intending to get in close and mix it again.

Without pausing to think, Dan rolled swiftly on to his side, heard the wicked thud of the knife as it struck the deck where he had lain a few seconds before. The man gave a savage roar of anger, lunged forward to pluck the knife from the planks and use it again, but this time, Dan was ready for him. His upstretched hands caught at the other's boot, held on grimly as the man tried to shake himself free. Gradually, he succeeded in twisting the other's ankle around until the man screamed thinly, a high-pitched wail as pain lanced through his leg. He teetered for a moment, then fell off-balance.

Dan staggered up. His blurred eyes seemed to take a long time to focus on things about him. The other was already scrambling off his knees as Dan tried to make him out in the moonlight. The man's features were twisted into a mask of anger and pain and as he charged in, lips drawn back into a snarl that showed his teeth whitely in the shadow of his face, Dan swung, putting all of his weight and strength into the blow. The other emitted a faint bleat of pain, fell back and knowing that he had little time to finish the job, Dan crowded him, did not give him any chance to take the initiative again. His fists beat a solid tattoo on the man's face and chest. There was still a high-pitched ringing inside his head, but that no longer mattered. The man ended up near the rail, arms hanging loosely by his sides now, not having the strength to lift them now to defend himself, his mouth was hanging open and he swayed forward, head going down as Dan chopped hard on the back of the other's neck. The man gave a faint moan and collapsed at his feet, knocked out by the blow. Dan turned to throw a glance at the other man, but he still lay where he had fallen by the rails a couple of yards away.

Rubbing his hand over his sweat-glistening forehead, Dan stood by the rail for a long moment, drawing air down into his tortured lungs, shaking his head to clear it. The cool breeze that blew along the river eased the pain along his cheek a little where one of the other's blows had torn the skin and after a little while his vision cleared. He stared down at the two men lying at his feet. He had no sense of time as he stood there and he had no idea whether he had been leaning against the rail for one minute or ten. His flesh felt numb where the heavy fists of his attackers had hammered at him.

He heard the sudden, unmistakable click of a gun being cocked behind him. In spite of the tight hold he had clamped on his mind, there was an immediate stillness in him, holding him up taut. His head turned slowly and he saw the man who stood a little distance away, the rifle pointed in his direction.

'That was a damned good try, Carson,' said Tollinson softly. He took a couple of paces forward. 'Too bad it didn't work out. Now turn around!'

Reluctantly, Dan obeyed. His brain was working dully and it was difficult for him to think properly.

'You could make a lot of trouble for me, Carson,' muttered the other harshly. 'I guess I made a mistake telling you so much a few days ago. But now you're too close to New Orleans for me to feel comfortable about you. I'm going to have to do something about it.' He broke off suddenly and Dan guessed that if he was to save his life he would have to move fast. Moving his head, he swung his body sharply to one side, clutching at the rail and pulling himself away from the other, striving to turn to face Tollinson. He knew the other would not want to risk shooting him. The sound of a shot would carry far at that time of the night with only the sound of the engines and the paddles to drown it, and if it aroused the other passengers and the crew it could start a host of awkward questions for Tollinson.

He was half turned when the butt of the pistol hit him a stunning blow on the side of the head. Scarcely conscious, he slumped against the rail, feeling his fingers loosen in spite of the effort he put into retaining his grip on the cold, hard metal. His senses reeling, he saw the moonlight dim around him as his knees buckled weakly under him. For a moment, he hung there, fighting to remain conscious, utterly helpless. He knew that another blow would finish him but it never came. Instead, he felt strong hands grip him by the legs, heaving him up, over the side of the boat. It was impossible for him to summon up enough strength to resist. Vaguely, he was aware of Tollinson's face, grinning viciously, lit by the flooding moonlight, of the man's lips drawn back into a snarling grin of triumph, of the dark, glittering eyes, wide and staring as the other exerted all of his strength. Then he felt his body slipping clear of the rails, found himself falling through empty space.

The shock of hitting the water brought him swiftly to his senses. He went under, came up spluttering, his head pounding madly, heart thumping in his chest. The huge bulk of the paddle steamer blotted out the moon, a vast shape with a few lights still showing as it slid by. In his ears there was the tremendous throbbing note of the powerful engines and it came to him in a sudden flash of realization that unless he swam away from the boat he would be caught up in the swirling, raging maelstrom of the mighty paddles as they thundered the water into foam.

He was a strong swimmer but that blow on the head had made him groggy and he could feel the tremendous pull of the wheel as it bore down on him out of the night. Madly, he struck out for the distant bank, exerting all of his remaining strength as he fought the savage whirlpool set up by the churning paddles. Almost, it seemed that they would drag him back in spite of all his efforts. Then, slowly, he managed to pull away from the packet. His clothes were a sodden, dragging weight on his tired, bruised body. The bank still seemed as far away as ever in the yellow moonlight and whenever he paused and tried to touch bottom, his legs found nothing and he went under again, coughing and choking on the cold, muddy water as he surfaced.

Two minutes later, even though he was still some distance from the bank, his legs struck something hard and solid. For a moment, he floundered helplessly, then found his feet and clambered on to the low mudbank which lay submerged just below the surface. For a long time, Dan lay sprawled there, the water lapping around him. Through his blurred vision he made out the dark shape of the steamboat as it moved away around a bend in the river a quarter of a mile away. Then it was gone out of sight and he felt a shiver pass through him as the cold night breeze swirled about him. The moon was still high, throwing a wide yellow sheen on the water, marking off the dark trees on the bank, as a deep and impenetrable strip of midnight blackness. Slowly his breathing returned to normal. With an effort he managed to get to his feet and stand, swaying a little, struggling to stop himself from falling down out of sheer weakness. Reaction had set in. He estimated there was a stretch of more than fifty yards from the sandbank to the river's edge. But from here he would only have the current to fight and not the vicious undertow from the boat.

Numb and chilled, he marked the nearer shore, then slipped into the water again and struck out for it. His legs grew leaden, his clothing a weight that dragged him down and he wished now that he had kicked his boots off before leaving the sandbank. Fortunately, although he had been forced to leave his guns behind and most of his belongings, he still had the belt containing his money strapped around his middle.

When it seemed he could swim no further, his outstretched hands touched hard gravel and sand. Gasping painfully, he hauled himself up, dragging his body out of the water and over the edge of the bank with a wrenching of shoulder muscles, flopping face down in the long, coarse grass that grew beneath the trees, feeling all of the remaining strength drain from his weary body.

Presently he was able to sit up and take stock of his surroundings. Tall pine fringed the bank here and overhead the stars were bright and cold and remote, with only the sound of the river lapping along the bank and the wind making faint talk among the trees to disturb the long, lonely silence.

# 2

## Thunder in the Gunsmoke

After moving through the trees that fringed the mighty river, Dan camped out that night on a ledge which overlooked a broad table of barren, windswept land to the north of New Orleans. Here, the land was bony with spine-edged ridges and shot through with veins of ore that glittered faintly in the flooding moonlight, peopled with the upthrusting bushes and stunted trees and an occasional cluster of stubby oaks. The wind that had picked up during the early part of the night, continued unabated, holding through the rest of the night, sweeping unimpeded over the wide, rolling plain, bringing an icy and penetrating cold that forced Dan to lie huddled close to the fire, arms by his sides to keep in what little warmth there was in his body. There was little sleep for him during the night. His wet clothing dried slowly on his body and he felt the cold bite deep into his body, adding its own brand of aching pain to the bruises and cuts which he had sustained on board the ship.

He put his mind on Andrew Tollinson, feeling the deep-rooted anger act as an antidote to discomfort. He knew instinctively that he and the other would meet again and the next time he would ensure that he had the upper hand. At the moment, in spite of what the man had said, he wasn't sure what kind of business Tollinson carried on in New Orleans, apart from the fact that he had a cattle ranch nearby. That there was more to it than that, Dan felt certain. The other was evidently bringing in trained gunmen to help him and a thing like that always meant trouble.

Lying on the hard ground he listened to the wind prodding the harsh mesquite into crackling life, whining in and out of the narrow gullies which lay all around him. It still wanted another two or three hours to dawn and reluctantly, he forced himself to his feet and went over to the nearby bushes to gather more twigs for the fire, thrusting them on to the glowing embers, standing while the red sparks lifted high in the wind, new flames licking at the dry branches. Some night-hunting animal moved in a long lope through the bushes, paused for a brief moment on top of the distant ridge, a faintly-seen shadow that sent a little tremor of apprehension through him. He was out here in the middle of this wilderness without a gun to protect himself. There were not only animals to take into consideration, but men with the habits of animals. The Natchez Trace lay not far from this point, the hunting ground of the outlaw bands who lay in wait along it, for the travellers moving north from New Orleans, back into the distant State of Kentucky.

He sat there, by the fire, while the

moon continued its low, dipping glide towards the western horizon, and the cold grew more intense. His clothing was dry now, but there seemed to be a core of coldness deep within him that had nothing to do with the night and the sighing wind. He ought to have known that Tollinson intended to try to stop him from reaching New Orleans and starting trouble for him. When he heard that sound outside his cabin he should have been prepared for more trouble than those two men on deck. There seemed to be half a dozen things he might have done had he thought of them at the time and now he cursed himself for his folly. There was one good thing to have come out of this however, he told himself wryly. By now, Tollinson would be under the impression that he was dead, knocked unconscious, and drowned in the river. The physical drain of the night had left its mark on him, by the time the dawn finally brightened in the east; a pale grey light brightening slowly, dimming the stars in that direction, picking out the undulating nature of the territory. Getting stiffly to his feet, he began walking south, heading in the direction where he guessed New Orleans to lie.

★   ★   ★

Shortly after the sun rose, Dan found himself in a world of lush green grass interspersed here and there by outcrops of grey-blue rock. In the near distance, tiny hills lifted from the flatness of the plain and he halted on a small promontory to look about him. He reckoned he had walked almost five miles since setting out just after dawn from that small camp he had made in the desert country and his eyes were speculative as they surveyed the scene in front of him, the green slope which rolled out beneath him where it ran right up to the wide stretch of timber into which a narrow trail led, a grey scar against the green. He pushed his hair from his eyes, narrowing his gaze against the glare of the rising sun.

The deep silence which lay over everything seemed unbroken, with only the faint sigh of the wind as it rustled through the grass, bending gently in front of it. He craved a smoke to ease the tightness of his palate but had nothing with which to build one and tried to fight down the craving. Then he came suddenly alert, all thoughts of a cigarette forgotten as he heard the sound from the direction of the timber. An indistinct form broke out from one patch of trees and headed into another. Presently, more riders emerged, appeared for a brief instant as they cut out of the brushy hollow, heading after the first man.

Frowning, Dan stared down into the timber, then moved hastily down the slope, aware that there was something going on down there which seemed to be shaping up to what he knew this country to be really like. He had lost sight of the group by the time he reached the outer fringe of trees, but he guessed that as none of the riders had emerged from the timber, the first man had, in all probability, been caught by the pursuing riders. Here, being on foot, he made slow progress. The ground degenerated into sharp, knife-edged ridges and deep dips which he was forced to skirt. The gaunt, grey-branched trees clung tenaciously to the rough ground on the edge of the timber and thorn brush abounded at every turn, with long, snaking roots lifting themselves out of the hard-baked earth, threatening to trip him at every step. He moved on, not certain what he intended to do when he did meet up with these riders. Moving into the timber at an angle, he reached the narrow trail when he was well inside the trees, easing up a little now that he was hemmed in by the branches, knowing that he would not be able to move fast if he was discovered.

The rustling reached his ears a few minutes later, and dimly he was able to make out the gruff sound of voices in sharp conversation. As he moved forward, he heard a harsh question being asked, but it was impossible for him to pick out the words and then a man's voice snarled:

'You know what the boss said. Now let's get it over with and ride back to the ranch.'

'You won't get away with murder like this,' said another voice, taut and shaky. 'And if you figure that — '

'Shut up!' snapped the first man thinly, 'You had your chance to get out of the territory the easy way, but you decided not to go. Now it's too late for you to change your mind.'

Cautiously Dan inched his way through the thick brush. Parting it gently with one hand, he stared into the wide clearing. The scene which met his eyes was a grim one. The tall, thin-faced man had been pulled from his horse, which now stood only a couple of feet from where Dan was hidden. One of the men who crowded the other held a rope in his hands and even as Dan watched, it was sent snaking expertly over a branch just above the thin man's head, where it dangled down beside him, the noose swaying gently in the breeze.

It required no stretch of Dan's imagination to figure out what was going to take place in the very near future. This was evidently a lynching party, sent out by somebody to make sure that the thin-faced man was strung up and made no further trouble. The analogy to his own predicament on the paddle steamer came sharply into his mind and he felt a sudden sweep of anger in him. But there seemed to be nothing he could do. Certainly he couldn't —

Something drew his attention back to the horse immediately in front of him. For a moment, he wasn't sure what it was. Then he looked closer, saw the rifle in the other's scabbard. The men in the clearing were concentrating all of their attention on the man they were about to hang. Very slowly, Dan moved forward until he was beside the horse.

He felt it shy away from him as it sensed his presence, but it made no sound and it was the work of only a few seconds for him to slide the ancient rifle from the leather scabbard, easing it into his hands.

One of the men had reached up for the noose, was getting ready to drop it over the other's head and shoulders. A man gave a harsh laugh and the sound grated along Dan's nerves. Slowly, he stepped out of the brush into the clearing, the rifle held steadily in his hands.

'Hold it right there, man,' he said softly. 'Seems I've come into this deal at a rather interesting point.'

As one man, they swung to face him, freezing in surprise. At sight of Dan, the sweat-beaded face of the man with the noose around his neck twisted into a grimace of hope.

One of the men, a short, squat man, his face scarred down one cheek, edged his mount out of the circle, his glance hostile, as he said thinly: 'This is none

61

of your business, stranger. Now ride on out of here and leave things alone that don't concern you.'

Dan's lips twisted up into a hard smile and he moved the rifle very slightly so that it was trained on the other's chest. He saw the hardening of purpose in the man's eyes and said sharply: 'Make one false move towards your guns and you'll be the first of this bunch to die. Make no mistake about that. As for this being none of my business, I always like to see a man get an even break and as none of you seem to be wearing any badges, I reckon you ain't a posse.'

He glanced towards the man with the rope around his neck. 'What are they going to hang you for, mister? You don't look like a killer to me.'

'I've killed nobody,' said the other, his voice a kind of gasp as he tried to keep it from shaking.

'I believe you,' Dan said quietly. He did not remove his gaze from the hard-eyed man in front of him now, knowing inwardly that if he relaxed his vigilance for a single second, there would be a bullet on its way. He knew that the other riders backing this man up, were waiting only for a chance to draw, reckoning that it would not be possible for him to kill them all.

'Like I said before, mister,' grated the other hoarsely. 'Better you ride out and keep on riding. This *hombre* is a rustler and a thief. Out here, we string up men like that and no questions asked.'

'You're a liar,' said the thin-faced man harshly. He tried to ease his head from the noose, but his hands were tied behind his back and he could not do so.

Dan's gaze flickered to the man standing beside the other. 'You,' he said tightly, 'cut him free and get the noose from around his neck.'

The man tightened his lips. 'I'll be damned if I will,' he said defiantly.

Very slowly, Dan moved the gun. 'You'll be dead if you don't.' Sardonic amusement glittered in Dan's eyes and his finger tightened on the trigger, the knuckle standing out white under the skin. He saw the other swallow, look to the leader of this band as if for guidance.

'Stay where you are,' snapped the squat man. 'This *hombre* won't pull that trigger. We can call his bluff right now.'

His hand dropped towards the gun at his waist, but before the others rightly knew what was happening, the rifle in Dan's hands blasted smoke and thunder in the clearing and the other reeled back in the saddle, one hand clutching at his torn shoulder, the impact of the bullet almost knocking him clean from the saddle. He swayed forward, the stain of blood beginning to soak through his shirt and dribbling between his fingers.

'Are you going to be sensible now?' Dan asked, eyeing the man near the prisoner. 'Or do I have to put the next bullet in your heart?'

The other stared at him for a long moment, evidently trying to pluck up sufficient courage to defy him. Then with a snarl, he turned and cut the ropes which bound the other's wrists behind him, slipping the noose from around his neck before stepping away.

'Now you're showing some sense.' Dan nodded. He said to the man who was rubbing his chafed wrists: 'Get back there and on your horse. The rest of you get down and toss your guns into the bush.'

The man he had shot glared at him, his features corded and dark, suffused with anger. Then, reluctantly, he slid from the saddle, unbuckled his gunbelt with his good hand and threw it into the bushes. The rest of the men did likewise. Dan nodded, satisfied. Moving slowly forward, not once relaxing his vigilance, he picked himself out one of the horses, swung up into the saddle, said quietly:

'You mounted up, mister?'

'Yeah,' answered the other from behind him.

'Right. Then ride on out of here. I'll

be right behind you.' Dan heard the other swing his horse, then ride into the brush. He waited until the beat of hooves had faded a little, then swung his mount, urging the rest of the horses in front of him. A sharp gunshot from the rifle spooked the horses, sent them stampeding from the clearing into the timber, scattered them far and wide. There was little chance of any pursuit now, he told himself as he rode swiftly from the clearing.

Reaching the edge of the timber, he glanced ahead of him, made out the other man a mile in front of him, and spurred his own mount after him. Every nerve in him was drawn taut, even though he knew there would be no men riding after him. He caught up with the other a couple of miles further on. The man was sweating and red-faced and he kept glancing apprehensively behind him.

'No need to worry,' Dan told him. 'I scared off their horses. They'll have to walk it back from wherever they came.'

'Tollinson's ranch,' said the other shortly. He reined his mount up beside Dan's as they reached a small stream. Leaning sideways in the saddle, he held out a calloused hand. 'I haven't thanked you for saving my life back there, mister. The name's Callard. Jem Callard. I own a small ranch and a piece of land a few miles west of here. You're welcome to food and shelter if you need it.' He let his gaze wander over Dan's clothes, the stubble on his face.

'Thanks. I guess I am hungry.' Dan grasped the other's hand, feeling the strength in it. Here, he thought, was a man who had been forced to work hard for everything he had got.

A short ride over the wide hills brought them to the trim, log-built ranch that lay in a hollow fold in the ground. A small creek flowed within a few yards of it, splashed over a stretch of flat rock before meandering over the smooth grassland, where several head of cattle were browsing peacefully. There were half a dozen horses in the small circular corral in front of the courtyard. Reining up in front of the house, Callard slid from the saddle, opened the wooden gate and let his mount into the corral, motioning to Dan to do likewise.

'Well, what do you think of the place?'

Dan glanced around him, nodded approvingly. 'Pretty good, Callard,' he acknowledged. 'Is this why those *hombres* back there were trying to string you up? Because of this small spread you've got here?'

'You've guessed right first time,' said the other grimly as he led the way on to the porch and then into the coolness of the small parlour. Glancing about him, Dan saw no sign of a woman's hand here, although he had more than half expected it. The other must have seen his look, for he said quietly: 'My wife died three years ago. She's buried up there on the knoll. We never had any children and I look after myself now.'

Noticing the shadow that came to

Callard's face, Dan said seriously: 'I'd have figured that you would have been only too willing to sell out and move back east in those circumstances.'

'Maybe so,' said the other shortly. He went into the kitchen adjoining the parlour and Dan heard him fiddling with pans and cutlery. From the kitchen, the other's voice reached him. 'Trouble is, I never liked selling out to a crook like Tollinson. He offered me less than rock bottom price for everything here, knew that if I didn't accept, he could get it by running me out of the territory, or sending his men out to string me up like they did this morning. If you hadn't happened along when you did, he would have been able to take over the ranch without any trouble and without having to pay a penny for it.'

'I get the picture,' Dan said grimly. It was one of the often told stories along this stretch of the frontier. In the beginning, the big ranchers had been jealous of the small settlers who moved in on land granted to them by the

Government. They had considered this country to belong to them. They knew it better than the settlers knew their own faces, they had ridden this land when it had belonged only to the Indians and the herds of buffalo. Now they saw it being divided up into small plots of land by men who merely scratched at the soil, stringing their barbed wire over the wide trails, making it impossible to drive the vast herds of cattle across the territory.

Callard came in with plates of beans, sweet potatoes and bacon. A large pot of scalding coffee followed and then he pulled up his chair to the table and sat opposite Dan. Even while they ate, Dan noticed that the other kept watching intently through the window that opened out on to the rolling hills just beyond the courtyard. Clearly the other was still unsure of himself, still apprehensive, knowing that the chips were stacked against him and that although good luck had been with him on this occasion, his luck might well be out the next time that Tollinson made an attempt to get rid of him.

And there would be a next time, Dan thought grimly. A man like Tollinson never gave up. No matter how many attempts he had to make, he would continue to do so until Callard was dead or out of the country.

'You know that Tollinson will be coming again, don't you?' he said finally, sitting back and sipping the coffee. He felt better now that he had eaten and allayed the biting pangs of hunger in his stomach which had been troubling him ever since he had swum ashore from that steamer.

'He'll come,' said Callard, speaking through his tightly clenched teeth. 'And when he hears what you did, he'll be on your trail too. Nobody stands up to Andrew Tollinson and gets away with it. He's too big a man in these parts. They reckon he owns nearly half of New Orleans and most of the land on either side of this part of the Natchez Trace. That's why he wants this spread. He can't abide to see settlers moving in on this territory.'

Dan nodded. 'Tell me, is Tollinson's place far from here?'

'About twenty miles out of New Orleans, along to the West. About forty from here.' He finished his coffee, frowned down at the empty cup for a long moment, then got to his feet and walked over to the window. 'This is none of your quarrel,' he said at last, not turning as he spoke. 'Better keep on riding to wherever you were headed when you met up with me, and forget that any of this ever happened. That way, you might at least stay alive so long as you're in this neck of the woods.'

Dan's eyes moved to the other. 'Maybe it is my business,' he said softly. He watched as the other swung on him sharply, a curious expression on his face. He gave a tight grin. 'I've already met up with Tollinson. I have a score to settle with him. One that won't wait.'

A sudden gleam came into Callard's eyes. He gave a quick nod. 'I figured there might be something like that. You half gave yourself away when I mentioned his name. You want to stay here for a while? Plenty of room now and a man gets a mite lonely out here by himself.'

'Thanks. But I reckon I'll ride on into town and take a look around the place, keep my eyes and ears open.'

'You'll need guns if you're going to tangle with Tollinson and his men,' said the other, eyeing Dan's empty holsters.

'I reckon I can buy a pair in town,' Dan said.

'And if they're waiting for you somewhere along the Trace, you'd never have a chance.' The other turned and went out of the room. He came back a moment later with two pistols which he handed to Dan. 'Take these. They'll be better than nothing until you can get a pair for yourself.'

Dan thrust the guns into his holsters, nodded slowly. 'I'll take that outlaw's mount,' he said tightly. 'I reckon there's still plenty of wind left in him and it might be that if they spot the horse in town they might come looking for me and save me the trouble of trying to find them.'

Callard's mouth thinned into a hard, tight line. 'Ride slow and easy when you get to New Orleans,' he warned. A gust of expression passed over his face. 'All strangers riding in there are watched. It's a hell of a town with every man walking around, watching everybody else, wondering when something is going to break. And when it does there'll be one almighty blow-up, the likes of which they've never seen before.'

'I'll remember,' Dan said. He moved to the door. 'And thanks for the grub. It was just what I needed.'

'Only too glad to be able to repay you in some way,' said the other. He eyed Dan closely. 'Don't forget what I told you. Watch your step all the way. If Tollinson or his men get a decent bead on you, they'll shoot you down — preferably in the back. That's the way they work.'

Dan went into the corral and cornered the bay horse, the saddle still on it, pausing only to tighten the cinch under the animal's belly before climbing up into the saddle. There was still some residual stiffness left in his body and he thrust his legs down straight against the stirrups in an attempt to ease it a little. A few moments later he rode out of the hollow and cut up south into the low hills which surrounded the small spread. Inwardly he felt a sense of concern about Callard. Tollinson would waste no time once he learned that his early plan to eliminate the other had failed.

Maybe that night his men would ride out to the ranch, determined that this time there would be no mistake, nobody to step in and help Callard.

Once over the low hills, Dan rode cautiously, eyes alert for any sign of trouble, scanning the country that lay around him. There was no knowing how far those outlaws had gone and if they had managed to round up their horses, they would be riding out after him, knowing that he intended to follow Callard to his ranch. He tried to think of a plan to put into operation once he reached New Orleans. There ought to be some kind of law in a town of that size and importance, he reflected; and yet if Tollinson was as powerful and influential as Callard had maintained, and as he had guessed for himself during their meeting on the river boat, the chances were pretty good that he might have the law in his pocket too. It had been known to happen on many occasions and there seemed no reason to suppose that the Marshal in New Orleans was any different from some of the crooked lawmen that Dan had known in the past.

His thoughts were still on Tollinson when he rode into a narrow canyon that had been cut by nature out of the solid rock. The walls rose sheer on either side to a height of more than two hundred feet, towering above the trail as it wound and twisted its way through them. He felt a growing apprehension as the rocky walls hemmed him in. If there was to be any bushwhacking done on the trail into New Orleans, this was evidently the logical place for it to be carried out. He tightened his lips, scanned the rocky ledges above him on both sides of the trail. The sunlight, striking obliquely down into the canyon, only managed to touch the uppermost reach of the sheer rock, giving it a deep red tint, with the rest in deep shadow. He was halfway through the canyon when he heard the faint abrasion of sound in the distance at his back, heading towards him, growing louder as the riders approached. He cast about him quickly for some place to pull off the trail and take cover until they had gone past, knowing that even this ruse might not succeed as the dust of his ride must surely be still in the air, getting into their nostrils and warning them of his presence directly ahead of them. But it was the only chance he had.

He touched spurs to his mount's flanks, urged it on swiftly. The horse leapt forward dispiritedly, feet striking the rocky floor of the canyon with a hard, ringing metallic sound. A little while later the rocky walls began to drop down beside him and he urged the flagging horse to a quicker pace, forcing it along the rising incline, sorry for the mount as he did so, but knowing that he had to get out of this canyon before those approaching riders caught up with him.

Wind and sand had scoured and abraded the walls of the canyon here and a hundred yards further on there was a narrow gap in the near side wall, leading out on to a level stretch of ground. Without pausing to think he put his horse through the gap, felt his legs scrape roughly on the sandstone. Then they were through and he backed off on the reins, let the pressure go, moved the horse slowly away from the opening and bent forward in the saddle, holding his hand over the animal's nostrils to prevent it from making any sound when the other horses came by.

He listened to the horses come on, interest and caution blended together in his mind. Sound and riders came quickly around the bend in the canyon trail, reached abreast of the gap, and then passed on. He heard the steady tattoo of hooves on the trail, moving out into the open country that lay beyond. Edging his mount right up to the rear of the canyon wall at this point, he held it tightly in to the warm sandstone as he caught a glimpse of the tightly-bunched group of men just visible in the cloud of dust kicked up by their horses. He did not doubt that it was the same bunch that had attempted to string up Callard, and he could easily figure out where they were headed. To report back to Tollinson what had happened. The other would either be in New Orleans or out at the ranch, but whichever it was, they would soon find him and give him the news.

He rode back on to the trail and followed the others, taking care to remain some distance behind.

★ ★ ★

Jennifer King reined up the wagon before the hotel and went inside. She had already seen Aaron Lewis and impressed on him her determination to carry on in New Orleans where her father had left off, had listened to his persuasive arguments against this and had put forward her own, ignoring his pleas that she should forget all about this crazy, and possibly dangerous, notion and resign herself to the fact that nobody was big enough or strong enough to stand up to Andrew Tollinson, that already, the other was bringing in more hired gunhands to make sure that his word was law and that nobody else tried to fight against him.

All of this had not impressed her. Had it not been for the fact that she felt absolutely certain that it was Tollinson who had ordered her father's killing, she might have been prepared to listen to Aaron. She had known him all her life, knew that he wanted her to marry him and often toyed with the idea that sooner or later she would say yes. But her father's death had changed all of this drastically. Now she had only one thought uppermost in her mind; to destroy the man who had murdered her father, even if he had not been actually present when he had been killed. She meant to do this by every means at her disposal.

Slowly, she made her way up to her room. Inwardly, she felt a little troubled. She had been near to quarrelling outright with Aaron and the thought had hurt her. She knew that there had been a great deal of wisdom in what he had said, but her hatred of Tollinson and all that he had done, all that he stood for, had made her blind to his arguments. Inside her room, she went over to the window and looked down on to the street below. A river boat had just tied up at the levee judging by the noise and bustle outside, with dozens of negro women and children making their way down to the quay.

The air in the room felt oppressively warm even though the window was open and she drew a deep breath inside her, then narrowed her eyes as a small group of riders swung into view at the far end of the street and rode slowly towards the hotel. They reined in front of the building and she felt her breath tighten in her lungs as she recognized Andrew Tollinson. She drew herself back from the window, fingers clenched so tightly that her nails dug deep into the palms of her hands, although she scarcely noticed the pain.

When the knock came to her door, her lips moved close together, but the tense feeling of excitement passed and when she opened the door to Andrew Tollinson, she was completely composed.

'I hope you'll forgive me calling on you like this, Miss Jennifer,' said the other, smiling slightly. He held his hat in his hand, looked beyond her for a moment into the room, then made a gesture with the wide-brimmed hat. 'Do you mind if I come inside? I'd like to talk with you if I may.'

Jennifer hesitated for a moment, her thoughts racing, wondering what the other had on his mind, why he had come to see her. Then she said sharply: 'Come inside, Mr Tollinson and speak your piece,' and turned back. She walked into the room and stood over by the table, watching as the other came in and closed the door gently behind him.

Tollinson smiled in a friendly way, showing his white teeth as if he were proud of them. 'First of all, I'd like to say how sorry I am about your father's death,' Tollinson shrugged slightly. 'It must have been a terrible blow to you.'

'It was.' There was no question of Jennifer's feelings; she showed her dislike, her hatred even, of the other on her face, revealed it when she spoke, 'I know quite well that he was murdered and I intend to find out who killed him and then I'll decide what to do about his killers.'

Tollinson lifted his brows in mute surprise. 'I'm afraid I don't quite understand you. I heard from the Marshal that it had been an accident, that he must've knocked the lamp from the table and the fire prevented him from getting out.'

'Then I'm afraid that the Marshal must have been lying to you, Mr Tollinson,' Jennifer said. 'My father was deliberately murdered. The press had been smashed and thrown over on to its side and it would have taken two men at least to have even moved it. And judging from the way in which the offices went up, there must have been oil all over the floor when the fire started. Whoever killed him, was not very clever in covering up the evidence.'

Tollinson frowned. 'Then in that case, I can quite understand your feelings. I trust that if there is anything I can do to be of any help to you at this time, you'll feel free to call on me, either here or at the ranch. I shall be only too pleased to do whatever I can until you've decided what to do, whether to stay in New Orleans or go back East.'

Jennifer smiled tightly, facing the other over the table. 'Somehow, I doubt if you'll be so ready to help me when you hear what I have decided to do. I've already had a word with Aaron Lewis. I mean to reopen the newspaper office and begin printing The Courier again. And when I do, I shall print the same sort of articles my father did. Perhaps mine may be a little more to the point and backed up by more evidence than his were.'

Tollinson stared at her, revealing nothing in his gaze. Then a change came to his face. His lips tightened and the friendliness went out of his eyes.

'You're being a bigger fool than I took you for,' he said throatily. 'What do you expect to gain by fighting me? Your father tried it, although I warned him repeatedly against it. Now you think that you can take up his cross and drive me out of this territory.' He shook his head vehemently. 'You can't do it. Nobody can stop me and you know it. So why waste your time and make things more dangerous and difficult for yourself?'

'You don't frighten me, any more than you frightened my father. You had to kill him to stop him. Maybe you think that you'll do the same with me.'

A gleam came into the other's eyes. He took a step forward, hands gripping the edge of the table tightly, then he took a hold on himself, checked any move he might have had in mind. 'When a man has built an empire with only his gun and his hands to back him up, he'll do anything to hold on to it. You should know that, Jennifer. That's what it's like with me.'

'And you would murder to keep what you've got?'

'If it should prove necessary.'

A deep anger showed on the girl's face. She said tautly: 'So you admit that you had my father killed?'

Tollinson shook his head. 'I admit nothing and you'll never be able to prove anything. My advice to you, young lady, is to go back East where you belong and forget everything about this place. Otherwise, believe me, you'll regret it. I suppose that this lawyer friend of yours put you up to this idea?'

'Aaron knew nothing about it,' declared the girl harshly. 'He has tried to talk me out of it but I've refused to listen to him.'

'I see.' Tollinson rubbed his chin. 'It seems that this lawyer has more sense than you have. You would do well to listen to him and take his advice.'

Facing him squarely, Jennifer said thinly: 'Somehow I have the feeling that you're not as sure of yourself now as you want me to think. You're wondering what harm I can do if I carry out my threat of starting up the paper again, and you're trying to figure out how to stop me without making it too obvious this time.'

Tollinson watched her steadily for a long moment, holding her with his eyes. Then he said sharply: 'Remember what I've said. I don't want to have to bring you any further trouble, but I will if you push me too far. This town is no place for you. Go back where you belong, where you'll be safe.'

Turning, he gave her no chance to add anything more. Opening the door, he stepped out into the corridor, closed the door behind him. Jennifer stood stock still in the middle of the room, listening to the faint sound of his footsteps fading into the distance as he walked down the stairs and into the lobby below. She felt suddenly weary to the bone from the effect of that meeting. She had stood up to Tollinson, had met the iron that was in him with her own and now there was the feeling of letdown in her, the inevitable reaction setting in as she tried to think things over in her mind, wondering what to do now. She did not doubt that Tollinson would do everything in his power to stop her from going through with her plan to start up the newspaper once more. He would have recognized that she meant every word she had said; and he would have realized that she could, perhaps, prove to be a far stronger force against him and his plans than her father had been. There were people in this town who would have been asking themselves questions about the death of her father and if she came out with some of the evidence, they would realize just what sort of people they were up against and they might be more willing to take some form of action.

Sighing, she sank down into one of the chairs near the window, glancing out into the sunlit street. Tollinson had met up with the rest of his men outside the hotel and she could just glimpse him as he climbed into the saddle, said something to the man nearest him, then jerked his horse's head with an unnecessary roughness, leading the men along the street in the direction of the saloon. For a moment, she debated whether to tell Aaron about this meeting, and then decided against it for the time being. It would only strengthen his resolve to get her to forget her wild idea if he realized there would be some definite danger to her.

As she sat there she felt her attention drawn to a lone rider who had just come into sight at the far end of the street and who was jogging his mount in the direction of the hotel. He sat tall and loose-limbed in the saddle and her gaze took in the guns strapped low on his hips, the rugged features and the level grey eyes that took in everything as he rode slowly in her direction.

She wasn't quite sure what it was about the other that attracted her attention to him so strongly. Certainly, he was the kind of man one would instinctively have picked out in a crowd of men, the sort of man who looked as though he were capable of looking after himself, a man not afraid of trouble, willing to meet it more than halfway if he had to.

She rose from her seat and watched as he slid from the saddle, tethering the horse in front of the hotel before stepping inside. Just what sort of a man was he? she wondered inwardly. Another drifter, riding through — or a hired gunfighter, brought in by Tollinson to help him drive the settlers from their ground along the Trace? She felt a faint feeling of alarm build up inside her as that thought went through her mind, then instantly thrust it away. He did not look the sort of man who would sell his gun to the highest bidder as most of the men who worked for Tollinson had evidently done. They were men one jump ahead of the law, safe so long as they worked for Tollinson and did all of his dirty chores for him, knowing that if they tried to run out on him, that immunity would instantly be withdrawn and they would be on the run again, with every man's hand against them.

* * *

In the lobby of the hotel, Dan paid for his room in advance, went up to it to leave what few things he had, then came down again and waited while the clerk sent someone to draw a hot bath for him. He felt bone-weary from lack of sleep and the long ride that morning, his bruised body aching in every limb. When the bath was ready, he stepped into it and allowed the warmth and the well-being to seep back into his bones and loosen his muscles so that he was able to relax fully and completely for the first time in several days. It was an excellent feeling, one which he had not expected to experience again.

Back in his room he put on his shirt again after knocking most of the dry dust from it, buckled the money belt around his middle once more, then poured some water from the pitcher

92

into the cup on the small table and drank his fill of the cool, though brackish, water. His face burned where it had been scorched by the sun and the hot wind but he felt relaxed as he rolled a smoke with the tobacco and paper he had bought on his way into town. Lighting it, he drew the smoke gratefully into his lungs, fully enjoying the feeling of utter laziness that was in him. He knew that Tollinson was probably somewhere in town and that once the other read his name in the register, or had it brought to his attention by the clerk — as seemed probable — the other might come looking for him.

He decided not to dwell on that possibility until he had eaten. Going out of the room he moved along the short corridor, down the stairs and into the dining room. He ate his meal when it came, realizing how ravenous he was, washed it down with hot coffee, then leaned back in his chair and rolled himself a smoke. The bath had eased the tension in him, had soothed away the pain of bruised limbs and the hard, scorching touch of the sun. Now he felt relaxed and lazy, enjoying the luxury which came after the meal. But at times, as he smoked the cigarette, he felt the restlessness beginning to boil within him, guessed that Tollinson would not be far away, might even be looking for him at that moment; and the thought was a faintly disturbing influence in his mind.

At the moment he had no plan of campaign. He knew the utter foolishness of trying to tangle outright with a man of Tollinson's stature here on his own stamping ground. He would have to play his hand very carefully, learn all he could about the other, try to discover how things were here in New Orleans or even out along the Trace itself.

As he sat there, he found himself musing on the stories he had heard of the infamous Natchez Trace, that overland trail which led from New

Orleans, on to Natchez and then up into Kentucky territory. Perhaps the most-used trail in the whole of the western frontier at this time, it had always had a bloody history, a name for outlawry and murder, of the gangs who lay in wait for the rivermen, the politicians and the gamblers who moved back along it after coming down-river to New Orleans. Most of the way it ran through cane where it was difficult for two men to ride abreast and across some of the worst country in the territory.

Was this man Tollinson in cahoots with these outlaws who roamed this trail? It seemed likely. It was seldom that a man gained a position such as Tollinson had now without being ruthless and somewhat dishonest. The point seemed to be that some were more dishonest than others and judging by the men Tollinson had gathered about him, he had probably strayed over the border of the law on several occasions and was considering doing it again in the future. If a full scale range war broke out along the Trace, with the settlers on one side and men like Tollinson on the other, it could prove to be the bloodiest battle in the history of the West.

Going out into the street, he untethered the horse, walked it to the nearby livery stables. A man drifted out of the dimness at the rear, glanced at the horse, then eyed Dan curiously, a bright glitter in his deep-set eyes.

'You a stranger here, mister?' he asked pointedly. There seemed to be a little more to his question than just an attempt to be friendly.

'That's right.' Dan nodded, handed the bridle to the other. 'See that he's fed and watered.' He handed a coin to the groom. The other took it and stared down at it for a long moment, then looked back at the horse.

'Seems to me I've seen this critter before,' he said softly. 'Could be I'm mistaken but it sure looks like Clem Harper's mount.'

'Reckon you're mistaken,' Dan said easily. He moved out into the sunlight, paused at the entrance to the stables, glanced back. The man was still standing there, holding on to the reins, eyeing him with a faintly puzzled glance. Then he seemed to catch at himself abruptly, swung on his heel and moved off into the rear of the stables.

The man was obviously suspicious and would probably make a point of seeking out this Clem Harper. If he did, so much the better. It would bring things to a head all the quicker. Making his way over to the saloon which stood pressed between two taller buildings on the opposite side of the street, Dan thrust open the doors and went inside. It was cooler here, out of the glare of the sun. Lifting one finger, he laid his elbows on the bar and rested his weight on them. All at once he felt better than he had for a long time past. Now at least, he knew something of what he was up against and the feeling of tight excitement was riding high in him. For a moment he wondered about the woman he had glimpsed just as he had ridden into the street and paused in front of the hotel. She had been glancing down at him from one of the upper windows, watching him, he knew, with a frank interest and curiosity. There had been something about her which had struck him forcibly, although at the moment, it was something he could not put a name to. The barkeep moved forward, paused in front of him, then dug below the counter and brought out a bottle and glass, set them on the bar in front of Dan as the other gave a quick, brief nod in answer to the man's inquiring glance.

'You look like a man who's travelled some distance,' the other said, his glance meeting Dan's head-on.

'Some.' Turning slightly, Dan allowed his gaze to run over the other men in the saloon. There was a small group of them in one corner playing cards, while several others were leaning against the bar a few yards away, drinking and talking softly among themselves. One man stood against the small window which looked out on to the street. He seemed to be watching for something and Dan felt his gaze drawn to the other. The man at the window turned sharply, as though feeling Dan's glance on him. He was short, stockily-built, with a dark, bristle-sharp moustache and gimlet eyes that seemed to bore into Dan as he returned his stare.

He came forward and almost immediately the group at the bar turned as one man and watched what was going on. Dan felt a sudden rise of interest. Turning back, he poured himself a drink, drained it quickly, keeping an eye on the other through the mirror that ran along the whole length of the bar at the back

'I noticed you ride over to the livery stables, mister.' Tension seemed to have tightened the man's voice. 'That horse you were riding looks mighty familiar to me. Where'd you get him?'

Dan turned slowly, let his glance run

idly, almost insolently, over the other as if appraising him. He knew that the men playing cards had also stopped their game and were staring in his direction and that the barkeep had stepped back a couple of paces.

'You seem to be mighty interested in my horse,' Dan said softly, with no emotion in his tone.

'Your horse?' This time, there was a note of menace in the man's tone, his voice very soft. 'From what I saw, it looked to me like Clem Harper's horse. He had it stolen by some *hombre* who butted in this morning when there was a little matter of justice being carried out.'

So these were some of the men who had been in that lynching party, Dan thought swiftly. He had not recognized them, simply because there had been so many in that large clearing and he had had time to notice only those who represented danger at the time. He wondered where the others were, then put the thought from his mind. He had to live with the present at the moment. He did not doubt that this man had recognized him, as had the others at the card table, although he wasn't sure about the other men along the bar. With an effort he forced the clawing fingers of tension in his body to relax. This would have to be played carefully and coolly.

'Could be that you've made a mistake.'

The other's eyes shone with hate. 'You're talking wrong this time, mister. Ain't no mistake, unless you're the one who's just made it. You figure I don't recognize you?' He thinned his lips into a hard line. 'Never thought you'd be foolish enough to ride on into New Orleans afterwards.'

The other watched Dan much in the same way that a snake watches a rabbit, unblinkingly, not a muscle of his face moving under the dark skin. He seemed to be waiting for the right opportunity to strike, to go for his gun and shoot down this man who stood in front of him, possibly knowing that some of the others in the saloon would also back him up the minute he made his play.

'You thinking of doing something about it?'

A sudden look of anger came into the gunman's face. His eyes grew flinty. Stepping back a little, moving away from the bar so that he would be able to draw, he said tightly. 'Mister, I reckon I'd be doing Mr Tollinson a favour knocking you off. I'm going to call you.'

Dan eased himself slowly away from the bar. He let his glance flicker for a moment towards the four men at the card table, noticed that they had also got to their feet and were standing away from the table, their eyes on him, faces hard, their hands swinging loosely by their sides.

'You always call a man with four other men standing at your back, ready to draw?' he asked softly. 'Seems to me you're not quite sure of this. I reckon it could be that you're a mite scared and — '

'Damn you, quit the talk and move away from the bar, and the minute you do you'd better go for your guns.'

Dan edged slowly from the bar, his gaze deliberately unfocused so that he was able to take in the shapes of the men at the back of the room too. They had not fanned out as he had expected them to and he guessed they felt certain that this man who faced him would be able to take him; and it would only be in the very unlikely event of him not being able to that they would have to join in the fight.

Teeth bared in a snarl, the other stood with his legs braced well apart, his hot, angry gaze on Dan's face, his breath coming through his parted lips in short, hard gulps. The bartender was edged right at the rear of the bar now, his face white, his eyes wide and staring. Dan watched the man's eyes in front of him, knew that here was a man who felt confident in himself that he could beat the man facing him to the draw. He would give away the moment when he intended to go for his gun by the change of expression in his eyes.

Sweat had broken out on the other's forehead and was trickling down his cheeks and the sides of his nose. Dan felt the tension heighten inside the saloon. The slightest sound or movement would set the guns blasting. The other stood it for as long as he could and then with a savage curse he heaved himself to one side, clawing for his gun. Before it had cleared leather, Dan's guns were in his hands and he triggered in the same smooth action.

The moustached man went back against the bar, striving to remain on his feet as the bullet tore into his chest. His gun slipped from his fingers and clattered at his feet and before his slack body had hit the floor, Dan's guns blasted again, the sound deafening inside the saloon. Two of the men at the card table reeled as their shoulders were caught by Dan's bullets. The other two men froze instantly, their hands touching the butts of their guns, now making no attempt to draw them.

The atrophying echoes had barely died away when the doors were thrown open and two men came into the saloon. One, with a badge glinting on his shirt, had a heavy pistol in his hand. He paused and glanced down at the man lying on the floor in front of the counter, then lifted his gaze to the other men standing stock still a few yards away, with Dan's guns on them.

'No more shooting in here,' called the marshal. He stepped forward, up to Dan. Now he had swung his gun to cover the other men. 'Put that gun away, mister. I'll take over from here. Who started this ruckus?'

'They did, Marshal.' The bartender had found his voice now and he regarded Dan with a look of awe on his florid features. 'It was Yates who called him, and the others joined in.'

Thorpe gave a quick nod. He bent and turned Yates over, then got to his feet with a heavy sigh. 'He's dead,' he said almost casually, as if he had expected nothing else. His cold glance rested on Dan. 'There aren't many men who could beat Yates to the draw,' he said appraisingly. 'You got some business in New Orleans?'

'Could be.'

'Then I'd sure like to know what it is. I don't aim to have your sort of man around, stirring up trouble. I've got enough here in town as it is without a gunhawk like you starting any more.'

Dan twisted his lips into a faint grin. He let his eyes rest momentarily on the men standing in a tight bunch, two of them nursing their shoulders. 'Seems to me that your gunmen are standing there,' he said softly. 'I didn't come into the saloon looking for trouble and I didn't start it.'

Thorpe gave him a bright-sharp glance. The expression on his face said that he considered there was a little more to Dan's statement than was apparent on the surface. He narrowed his eyes. 'I'd sure like to know what your business might be here. And it had better be good.'

Dan shook his head slowly. He holstered his guns, recognizing now that there was no danger from the other men at the moment. For a moment he let his glance flick beyond the marshal, to where the other man was standing, the man who had followed the lawman into the saloon. Well-dressed, wearing no guns, the other looked like a prosperous business man, possibly a merchant or a banker. He thought he saw a look of hostility in the man's eyes, but it was gone so quickly that he could not be sure.

'It's a good reason why I'm here, Marshal,' he said quietly, 'but it's a bad business.'

'Then I'm listening,' grunted the other harshly.

'I'm here to even the score with a man who tried to kill me,' he said evenly.

Thorpe lifted his brows sharply. There was a grimness on his face which could be clearly seen. 'What makes you think this man is here in New Orleans?'

'He's here all right,' Dan told him flatly. 'They tell me he's one of the biggest men in this part of the territory. His name's Andrew Tollinson.'

For a moment there was a long, tight silence in the saloon. Thorpe's lips had parted in sudden, stunned surprise. Then he gave a shaky laugh. 'You're not serious, mister. Why, you don't stand a chance. You've bucked some of his crew here right now, killed one of his best men. He won't let you get out of New Orleans alive and there's nothing I can do to help you.' He spoke as though he intended washing his hands of the whole matter now that Tollinson's name had been mentioned.

'I reckon I can see how things are, Marshal,' Dan said grimly. 'I've come across this situation before. The cattle-men put you in office here and if you want to keep this job, you do exactly as they say, and Tollinson speaks for all of the cattlemen. I don't suppose it matters to you that these men tried to hang a man this morning just because he refused to sell out to Tollinson.'

'These settlers have been warned often enough that they're not wanted in this country,' Thorpe said harshly. 'This is cattle country, to the west and north of New Orleans. If they want to settle any land, let them join the wagon trains and head west with the others. There's plenty of room for them out there. We don't want them stringing up their barbed wire across the trails. That's all Mr Tollinson is fighting against.'

'Is it?' Dan moved back to the bar and poured himself another drink, as if nothing had happened. His hand was rock steady as he turned to face the other. 'Seems to me that Tollinson is bringing in far more gunmen than he needs just to turn a few drifters off their land. He's got something bigger in mind than that. Maybe you know what it is and you're staying out of it, or you're as blind as all of the others. I've only been in this territory for a little while, but already I've seen enough to convince me of what he's after. The control of the entire Natchez Trace. Once he gets that in his hands he can make himself the boss of this whole area.'

He gulped down his drink, tossed a couple of coins on to the bar, then said to the marshal: 'If you want to talk about this little fracas any more, Marshal, I'll be somewhere around town or over in the hotel.'

He pushed himself past them, paused as he moved towards the door. The woman he had noticed at that window of the hotel was standing there, just inside the doorway. It was obvious that she had been there for a little while, had probably been listening to everything that had been said.

She brushed him with her glance as he stepped past her and he saw that there was something in it more than mere curiosity of him as a stranger. Her lips lay pressed softly together and it was as though she challenged him to speak to her, to break the indifference which lay in her.

Then he was out on the boardwalk, with the sunlight glaring in his face. He paused for a moment, rolled and lit a cigarette, drawing the smoke into his lungs. A moment later the woman's voice at his shoulder said: 'Walk over to the hotel, I want to talk to you.'

# 3

## Choice of Trail

Dan knew that the marshal's eyes were on him as he walked over the dusty road towards the hotel, the woman walking beside him, but he gave no sign of having noticed. He could guess at the thoughts which were running through the lawman's mind. Thorpe would be wondering when he was going to see the last of him, knowing for sure that he meant trouble so long as he stayed in New Orleans.

In this, he was right. No sooner had he disappeared into the lobby of the hotel than the marshal moved back into the saloon, said tersely to a couple of the men: 'All right, take Yates out of here and over to the mortuary. The others better cut along to Doc Moran's and get those shoulders attended to.'

While this was being done he turned to Aaron Lewis. 'What do you think of this man, Aaron? He could mean trouble if he decides to go ahead with his threat of gunning for Tollinson.'

'That's right, Marshal.' There was a puzzled frown on the other's handsome face. He glanced over the other's shoulder in the direction of the hotel. 'But what is worrying me is Jennifer's interest in him. She was standing there listening to all we said, I'm sure of it.'

'Then you think she may try to get him to help her?' The look of realization came into the lawman's eyes. 'You're right. She's been trying her darnedest to get Tollinson; she's sure he killed her father.'

'And this man is just the kind of reckless gunfighter who would throw in his lot with her if she asked him.' Aaron's mouth was suddenly dry. His mind was racing, wondering what was going on in the hotel that he knew nothing about. Was it possible that Jennifer would talk this gunman into

113

helping her destroy Tollinson and everything he stood for?

'She's got you worried,' Thorpe's toneless voice drawled.

'This whole business has got me worried,' growled the other, 'but I reckon I can cope.'

'Might be as well to warn Tollinson of what's happening,' murmured the other.

Thorpe stared at him in surprise. 'Just whose side are you on, Aaron?'

'I want to make sure that nothing happens to Jennifer,' declared the other. 'At the moment, she's set on doing everything she can to avenge her father's death and she won't listen to any of my arguments. She believes that Tollinson was the man behind her father's murder and unless she's stopped she'll end up as he did. But if I can warn Tollinson about this man, he'll take care of him pretty quickly and without him Jennifer will be able to do nothing.'

'I see what you mean.' Thorpe

rubbed his chin reflectively. His eyes were speculative. 'Reckon I might take a ride out there this evening.'

\* \* \*

Jennifer King gave Dan a studying glance and for a moment some indecision seemed balanced in her mind; then she shrugged her shoulders and said quietly:

'You'll have to be much more careful than you were over in the saloon just now. This town is on the brink of something big and dangerous and you've ridden right into the middle of it. I heard what you said back there. You want to kill Andrew Tollinson.'

'This seems to be kind of an uneasy town,' said Dan, ignoring her last question and what it implied. 'Has Tollinson got it that way?'

She smiled thinly. 'Not only the town but the whole of the Natchez Trace, clear to the Kentucky border. He's got his men riding that trail on the look out for men they can rob, settlers they can drive out of the territory. I've tried to get the townsfolk here to see what's happening, my father tried too but he was killed because he was getting too dangerous and troublesome.'

'And you think that Tollinson killed him?'

'Perhaps not directly, but he was the man who gave the order. He'd tried to frighten my father for some time, ever since he began to write and publish articles trying to tell everyone what Tollinson was doing, warning them that the same would happen to anyone who stood in Tollinson's way. Three months ago the offices were burned down and my father in them. The presses had been overturned and smashed beyond repair even if the fire hadn't damaged them.'

'And you want me to help you against Tollinson?' There was a directness to Dan's manner which the girl found vaguely disconcerting. She nodded her head slowly.

'I take you for a man who isn't afraid of Tollinson as the others are,' she countered.

Dan tightened his lips. 'Those men back there in the saloon. Were they part of the Tollinson outfit?'

'That's right. The man you shot, Yates, was a foreman at the ranch. In reality, he was a wanted killer.'

'And the marshal knew that?' asked Dan in mild surprise.

There was a mirthless smile on the girl's lips. She turned away from the window and sat down in one of the chairs. 'Of course, but here the law stands for nothing. Andrew Tollinson is the law in this part of the territory. Marshal Thorpe is only a figurehead and he knows it. He's elected by the cattlemen and to keep his job there he has to do as he's told, whether he likes it or not.'

'And who was that other man with the marshal?'

'Aaron Lewis. He's a lawyer in town.' A faint blush came to the girl's cheeks as she spoke. She hesitated for a moment, then went on in a tumbled rush of words. 'He's asked me to marry him on several occasions, especially since my father died.'

'And what views does he have? Do you know?'

'He thinks it's hopeless to try to fight Tollinson. He's tried to stop me from printing anything about him in the newspaper. I don't think he approves at all of what Tollinson is doing, but he won't stand up to him.'

'What about the settlers? If this is happening to them why don't they band together before it's too late? They must know that's the only way they can fight this thing before it overwhelms them all.'

'They're afraid of Tollinson. They've seen what happens to anyone who tries to resist.' She shook her head slowly. 'And it isn't only the settlers. The Trace is the only way back to Kentucky for most of the passengers and crews of the steamers which come downriver to

New Orleans. If this country is ever to grow, the Trace has got to be made safe for such people.'

'And you think I can help?'

'I'm not sure. You say that Tollinson tried to kill you. Isn't that enough for you to want to destroy him by any means?' There was a hardness in her voice, a look of hatred in her face that shocked him a little. He had not thought her to be a woman capable of such intensities.

'It could be,' he nodded musingly. He remembered the way Tollinson had hit him on the side of the head and then heaved his body into the river, leaving him to drown, fully expecting he would do so. The remembrance brought the surge of anger back into his mind, tightening the muscles of his chest and shoulders, forcing his hands to clench tightly, finger nails digging into the palms. He looked at her closely, standing wholly still.

'You're hard for a woman,' he said quietly. 'Though looking at you I don't think you were always like this.'

Her mouth tightened further. She seemed to think of that slowly, her mind reaching forward and forming around the thought, the truth of the matter coming to her in slow, easy stages. 'You're right,' she said at length. 'It was when my father was killed that I changed. But you know how it is too. I can see it in your face. You have this chore to do, haven't you?'

He nodded his head, puzzled a little. 'When it's done it's finished,' he said softly.

'You think so?' Her eyes challenged him directly. 'You really think that once you start gunfighting you can stop it any moment it pleases you?' She shook her head and the softness and a little of the sadness came into her face; he saw that she was a woman of courage and determination, afraid of little, but not willing to yield to softness when it came to anything that touched her directly. She had been deeply hurt by her father's death, but she had not allowed herself to give way to self-pity or tears. Instead, the experience had hardened her, made her bitter, deep inside. It would take a lot to ease all of that pain and misery and bitterness out of her soul, he reflected. Perhaps it might even be impossible for anyone — or anything — to do so.

Now she stood straight and tall before him and had her say. 'I noticed you when you first rode into town, although I didn't know then that Tollinson had tried to kill you. That's why I think you can help. Not only me, because of my father, but this whole territory. So long as this man is allowed to go on killing and plundering, bringing in more and more gunfighters to carry out his orders, there will be no peace in the country.' She paused and when she spoke again her voice was sharper. 'No man can go back on himself, or ride the same trail over again. But you'll try to do that, you'll fight until you're finished and you've evened the score. That's where you and I are so alike.'

'I'll do what I can,' he said eventually. 'So long as it doesn't interfere with what I've got in mind.'

'That's all I'm asking,' said the girl. 'But be careful. Particularly, keep your eye on the marshal. There's only one law here and that's for the cattlemen, with Tollinson making sure that it's administered his way.'

'And this lawyer fella? Can he be trusted?'

She hardened at the suggestion in his voice that Aaron Lewis might go over to Tollinson and had an instant answer. 'He won't help Tollinson in any way, although he may not fight him out-right.' She eyed him curiously. 'Does that make any difference?'

'It is entirely your business,' he said.

'But you disapprove of a man who can't stand up to what he thinks is right?'

'Hate to hear of a man who won't take it on him to fight when he comes up against something like this.'

She turned and looked fully at him. 'That's the most interesting and revealing thing you've said.'

Dan nodded, but said nothing. He waited for a moment and then, when the girl made no move to say anything further, he got to his feet and moved towards the window, glancing down over her shoulder into the street below. There was dust in the air, hanging over the street, dust lifted by riders heading out of town. He came instantly alert, watched the length of the street with a restless attention. There were several people on the slatted boardwalks, others in front of the saloon opposite the hotel. He lifted his gaze gradually, then without any warning, caught the girl around the waist and pulled her sharply to one side. The bullet struck the window and embedded itself in the wall at the rear of the room a split second before they heard the sharp, spiteful crack of the rifle.

'You all right?' he asked harshly.

She nodded, swallowed deeply, then

pushed herself upright, peering sideways through the broken window.

'Somebody wants you dead,' he said thinly, speaking through clenched teeth. 'I just caught the glimpse of sunlight on the rifle barrel a moment before he fired.' Carefully drawing a gun from its holster he edged his way forward, pushed his body tight against the wall at the side of the window, and risked a quick look across the street. The window from which the shot had been fired, on the upper storey of the saloon was empty now, although he fancied, for a second, that he saw a faint movement in the dim shadows of the room.

'Don't expose yourself at the window,' he said warningly. Swiftly he moved across the room, running down the stairs and out into the street. There were three men inside the saloon as he pushed through the doors, threw a swift glance about him, then headed for the wide stairway leading to the upper room. He heard the marshal yell after him but took no notice. Taking the stairs two at a time, he reached the top, drawn gun still in his hand. There was a wide corridor there with doors leading off on both sides of it. Quickly, he reckoned on which door led into the room from which that shot had been fired, twisted the handle and threw the door open. The room was empty, but there was still a faint blue haze and the smell of burnt powder hanging in the air and the window overlooking the street was open with a faint breeze blowing into the room.

There was nothing there to tell him who the bushwhacker might have been and he ran out into the corridor again, just as Marshal Thorpe and Aaron Lewis came pelting up the stairs.

'What's gotten into you?' demanded the marshal harshly. 'Running in here like a madman with a drawn gun.'

'Is there any way out of here except through the saloon at the front?' Dan spoke harshly, ignoring the other's question.

'There's a back stairs that leads into the alley at the rear.' said Thorpe. 'Was that a shot we heard from up here?'

'It sure was.' Dan ran to the far end of the corridor as he spoke, his tone grim. Even as he reached the end, spotted the narrow stairway that led down to the rear of the building, there was the sound of a horse being spurred savagely away from the saloon. Dan let his hand drop to his side. Thorpe came up to him, looked at him queerly.

'What happened?' he snapped hoarsely.

'Somebody tried to kill the girl,' Dan said tonelessly. He thrust the gun back into its holster. 'They fired from that room along the corridor.'

'Jennifer,' Lewis took a sharp step forward. 'Is she all right?'

'She's unhurt,' Dan told him. 'But whoever it was didn't mean her to stay alive much longer. He was sure shooting for keeps.'

'You see who it was?' Thorpe eyed him sharply.

'No. Though it doesn't take much

horse-sense to guess who it must have been.'

Lewis gave him a narrow-eyed glance. Turning to the marshal, he said: 'I figure this is your business. Better see if you can find anybody who saw what happened, see if anyone noticed that man who just rode away.'

Thorpe's brows went up into a tight line. 'You reckon anyone will talk if it was one of Tollinson's men did that shooting?'

'No, but it will give us something to go on. Whatever happens, of course, we can't accuse anybody without some evidence. It's no use blaming Tollinson, or his men unless we can pin something definite on them.'

'Now you're talking like a lawyer instead of a man,' Dan said harshly.

The other swung his gaze back to him. He paused for a moment as if debating Dan's statement, then he said: 'In the meantime I'd like to have a talk with you in my office.'

Dan shrugged: 'Seems to me that

everybody in this town wants to talk to me all of a sudden and I've only been in New Orleans a matter of an hour or so.'

'This could be important,' said the lawyer grimly. 'And it might be the means of saving your life.'

He turned, led the way down the stairs and out into the street, walking with the assurance of a man who knew that he would be obeyed without question. For a moment Dan felt a deep anger rise in him. Then he shrugged it away. If he was to learn anything at all about Andrew Tollinson and how the other operated, this was probably as good a way as any. He had to start somewhere and although the girl had given him something to go on, there were many more questions he would have liked answered.

Lewis led the way along the dusty street without once looking back to see if he was being followed. The smell of bitter dust still hung in the air. Dan could feel it stinging at the back of his nostrils, clogging his throat. Two hundred yards from the saloon Lewis paused in front of a small, but presentable, office. Unlocking the door, he pushed it open and waved Dan inside, closing the door behind him. The office was furnished austerely, with an oak table and three chairs and a red and blue carpet on the floor. Lewis went over to the other side of the room, poured a couple of drinks and brought them over, sinking down into the chair behind the desk. He waited until they had drunk before saying: 'You seem to have ridden right into the middle of big trouble.' Reaching into his drawer, he took out a small box of cigars, held it out to Dan, lit the one which the other took, thrusting it between his lips.

Blowing a cloud of smoke in front of his face he leaned back and said softly. 'Big trouble. At the moment, I'm not sure why you're here, whether you have something to settle with Tollinson that's quite apart from what is happening here, or whether you're just one of those men who ride the trails looking for trouble.'

'Does it matter?' Dan asked pointedly. He drew the smoke of the cigar deep into his lungs. 'Seems to me that this *hombre* Tollinson has got himself a heap of enemies, but nobody has the guts to stand up against him, so he's able to ride roughshod over the lot of you. And he'll go on doing that for as long as he likes.'

'There's no point in people getting themselves killed just for the sake of an ideal,' said the other, trying to sound reasonable.

'From what I hear, a lot of people are being killed if they refuse to sell out to Tollinson. I happened across one man this morning who was going to be strung up by a bunch of Tollinson's men.'

Lewis's eyes narrowed at that news, but he brushed it aside, almost as if it had no real importance to the subject they were discussing. That was the trouble with this man, Dan thought inwardly, he always seemed ready to talk over things as points of law; but once anyone started talking action, he backed down.

'You think we ought to start a range war out here?' Lewis chewed thoughtfully on the end of his cigar. 'You know what that would mean, of course. The end of what little law and order we have.'

'I always figured that the law was impartial, Mr Lewis. You're trying to tell me now that there's one law for the cattlemen and one for the settlers.'

Lewis leaned forward in his chair, rested his elbows on the desk. 'You have to see things our way. It's a case of which is the lesser of the two evils. Either hundreds of men die, or a handful of settlers, who ought to know better than to try to come here into cattle country, are run out of the territory.'

'I don't see it that way,' said Dan stiffly.

'You're entitled to your opinion, I suppose,' grunted the other. He straightened up. 'What did Jennifer King want with you?' His eyes bored into Dan's. 'I suppose she was trying to get you to help her in her feud against Tollinson.'

'She asked me to help,' Dan admitted.

'And you agreed?' There was a note of apprehensive interest in the other's voice.

'Not exactly. I came here to settle a score with Tollinson. If by doing that I help her, then it's all the same to me. But what I mean to do isn't for her, or for New Orleans, or the settlers along the Trace. It's for me.'

'I see.' Lewis got to his feet. He watched Dan with sharp eyes. 'If you start making trouble you may find yourself in jail — or six feet under the ground on Boot Hill.'

'I'll take that chance,' said Dan easily. He grinned a little as he got to his feet, stood for a moment with his hands on the back of the chair. 'As for making trouble, I reckon that Tollinson will be starting that when he hears about the gunfight in the saloon.'

He moved to the door, paused as he opened it, looked back. 'Thanks for the cigar,' he said quietly.

* * *

Dan had been two days on the Trace before he spotted any sign of trouble. Dark clouds had drawn in low over the land here and it was beginning to drizzle as he rode in among the cane stalks which grew thick and tall. Bullfrogs croaked dismally in the marshy ground that lay on either side of the Trace. In places the trail was so narrow that he could barely squeeze through, his knees scraping against the sharp cane. Maybe some day they would get around to making a proper road through this country, he reflected, as he rode; but that was still some years ahead. At the moment only horse and foot traffic used this part of the Trace as

133

far as Natchez, where it ran back in the direction of Nashville.

He had ridden for most of the day and all of the previous day without meeting anyone on the Trace. Sometimes, so he had heard back in New Orleans, it was possible for a man to ride for days without seeing any sign of life apart from the alligators that lived in the swamplands where the many tiny streams which flowered off the great Mississippi fanned out into the surrounding country.

He had considered his plans carefully since talking with Jennifer King and Aaron Lewis. He knew that Tollinson had been warned about his presence in New Orleans, possibly by the marshal, and he had decided against trying to have it out with the man openly. The chances of getting to Tollinson, with all of those hired gunslingers about him, were remote in the extreme. But if he could hurt the other in his attempts to dominate Natchez Trace, he might finally get the other so jumpy that he would make the kind of mistake Dan wanted him to make and then it would be the chance he was looking for.

At the top of a low rise he reined his mount and looked about him through the greyness of the drizzling rain. The canebrake continued for as far as the eye could see in almost every direction. Off to his right he saw that the brush grew heavier and the open country which lay there was cut off by rocky upthrusts. Except for a sudden rise of quail wings beating up into the wet heavens, and the grunting croak of the bullfrogs, the country about him seemed empty and lifeless.

He reckoned he had another day's travel before he reached Natchez, which meant he would be forced to make a wet camp that night, for there was no sign of any break in the weather, the sky grey and overcast right down to the horizons. Narrowing his eyes, he let the horse have its head. Down here, where the trail ran through the thick cane, it was easy to lose all sign of the Trace if one took the wrong turning and several times he was forced to backtrack, pulling the horse back on to the trail before continuing on again. He travelled steadily for more than two hours, ears alert, listening to the sounds all about him, picking out any which he did not recognize from the usual background noises, not content until he knew what they were. Once he heard the crashing of wild cattle in the brush, not too far distant and the bull-like roar of an alligator sent a little shiver through him as it sounded only a short distance away, the smacking crack as it moved through the water, shying his mount a little away from the sound.

Around a sharp bend in the trail he found a camping spot. The cane had been cleared for perhaps twenty feet around the place where the ashes were grey and wet and sitting high in the saddle, he judged that the fire was an old one. Shrugging a little, pulling up the collar of his jacket around his neck against the cold, biting wind, he rode on. He would be glad to get out of the cane. The three-inch thick stalks shut out all view of the surrounding country now that he was down among it and he felt hemmed in. He was used to the open spaces where a man could see right to the distant horizons whenever he rode, knew what lay out there for him; but here, danger could lie only a few inches away and a man would be unaware of it until it struck suddenly and without warning.

Presently he stopped his mount. Voices came from up ahead, carrying clearly in the stillness. He sat for a moment listening. Men on this trail were inclined to be a little jumpy, quick on the trigger whenever a stranger rode in among them, but he would have preferred company to camping alone that night. He could make out nothing of the conversation, the voices muffled by the cane. Gigging his mount, he rode forward, taking care to make plenty of noise to allay any suspicion on the part of the others. The trail turned a few hundred yards further on and he rode into a small clearing in the cane, very similar to that he had passed through an hour or so earlier.

There were two men seated around the fire which had been built in the centre of the clearing. One, a buck-shirted man with protruding teeth, looked up from the fire which sent up a spiral of grey smoke into the air, then he straightened and eyed Dan curiously. The man was quite tall and heavy, with a high-bridged nose and piercing grey eyes which fastened a coolly inhospitable glance on Dan's face.

'Company, Cal,' he said in a low voice as Dan reined his mount. A boy, barely nineteen, came out of the small lean-to, which had been hastily erected at the side of the trail, giving them a little shelter from the rain. A freshly-skinned deer lay on its side by the fire and there was a can of coffee bubbling over the flames, the aroma pinching Dan's mouth a little. For an instant

Dan noticed the lines of strain on the boy's features, then they relaxed as he swung down from the saddle.

'He don't look like one of them, Matt,' he said tautly.

'Where you from, mister?' asked the older man harshly.

'New Orleans,' said Dan easily. 'I'm riding through to Natchez. Smelled smoke and just followed my nose.'

The other nodded. 'We killed a deer a while back. You're welcome to camp with us for the night. We've got a place here out of the rain.' It was a grudging invitation, but nonetheless the other seemed to have accepted him for the moment. Dan hobbled his horse among the cane, knew that it might stray if he left it. He looked at the older man, called Matt, and met the steady onset of the man's impatient glance.

'I've got money. I can pay for my meal.' Dan hunkered down close to the fire, feeling some of the warmth seep into him.

'Not necessary,' said the other quietly. He let his gaze rest on the guns in Dan's belt. 'We've got plenty here.' He had a loose, easy way of speaking, and Dan guessed he was from Kentucky.

'You ridden this Trace before?' asked the boy. He put some small branches on to the fire in an attempt to liven it up. Gradually it began to show some red flame as the sticks and twigs caught.

Dan shook his head. 'Never been as far south as this,' he admitted. 'They tell me it can be unhealthy riding alone to Natchez.'

Matt eyed him sharply. 'There are plenty of men lying in wait for folk like us,' he acknowledged. 'If you got any money with you, I'd advise you to hide it somewhere out in the cane. A man can get himself killed just for the horse he's riding.'

'So I've heard.' He sat back as the boy speared a ham of the deer on a piece of wood, thrusting it through a tendon, then hung it over the fire. Dan rolled himself a smoke, then offered the tobacco to the others. They accepted it in silence and soon the appetising smell of cooking meat drifted on the air. An alligator roared in the swamp close at hand and the boy threw a quick, somewhat apprehensive look in the direction of the sound, lips tightening a little.

'They can smell the meat, I reckon,' Dan said casually. 'Must be hungry.'

'These critters are always hungry,' said Matt. He sucked hard at the damp cigarette, pulling the smoke down into his lungs. 'You say you've just ridden up from New Orleans.'

'That's right,' Dan nodded.

'You hear of a man named Tollinson while you were there?' Matt's eyes narrowed as he spoke. His gaze was a searching thing as he probed Dan's face, keen eyes missing nothing.

'Sure, I heard of him,' said the other casually. 'Big rancher, they told me. Owns several thousand head of cattle west of New Orleans.'

The boy glanced at him briefly, then

seated himself on the other side of the fire. He said shortly: 'We figured you might be one of his men. We know they watch this part of the Trace, ready to rob anybody they find.'

Dan smiled in a wintry way. He held out his hand for the cup of hot coffee which the older man handed to him. 'I fight for nobody but myself,' he said.

The reply seemed to satisfy the two men. They ate the deer ham while it was just warm. Dan did not mind eating it that way, and the other two seemed to enjoy it. He judged they were men from one of the riverboats, making their way back to Kentucky by the only overland route used by these men.

The food eased the gnawing pains in his stomach and by the time they were finished it was dusk. There was no sign of the sunset. The sun had been entirely hidden by clouds for two days and only a darkening of the grey overcast showed that night was coming on.

He checked his mount, then came back into the clearing. The boy had heaped more wood on to the fire and although it was too sodden to burn properly, the flames still caught deep in the heart of it.

'Reckon it should last until morning,' said Cal, nodding in satisfaction.

'You think it's wise to have a fire burning through the night?' Dan asked. 'If there are any outlaws in the vicinity, it'll attract 'em here. They might take us by surprise.'

'In this cane we ought to be able to hear 'em miles away, even if they try to ride quietly,' said Matt from inside the entrance of the crude lean-to.

'All right, if you reckon so.' Deep inside, Dan was not so sure. He knew that if he had had a mind to, he could have moved in on these two without being heard by either of them when he had approached along the trail. It had been quite wide a way back there just before it opened out into the clearing.

Inside the lean-to, there was more room than Dan had thought and he was able to stretch himself out on the cold ground, legs thrust out straight. The underside of the roof leaked a little, but it was better than being out in the rain and he put all thought of the discomfort from his mind as he stared up at the matted boughs, seeing just a little of the dark sky through them. The quiet breathing of the others told him they were asleep. Outside he could hear the quite soft movements of the horses in the cane, the faint crackle of it under their feet as they moved around a little restlessly. Maybe they would give them sufficient warning of trouble, he reflected, closing his eyes.

When he woke, it was still dark. His face was wet where drops of moisture had fallen on it from the roof of the lean-to and he eased himself up on to his arms quietly, straining his ears to pick out the sound which had wakened him, listening intently. There was no sound from the horses but he knew that he was not prone to wakening like this for no reason at all. Gently he got to his feet, stepped over the boy and moved like a ghost to the entrance of the lean-to, peering out into the wet darkness. The wind, which had sprung up earlier that evening, still made a creaking sound as it blew through the cane, a faint, eerie moaning that began to grate on his nerves.

Moving away from the clearing, he edged into the canebrake, circled away to the right, noiselessly. He was still not sure what had brought on this sudden sense of awareness, of danger; but he knew from past experience that it was something not to be ignored. He felt the tiny spot between his shoulder blades begin to itch as if someone in the shadowed cane were drawing a bead on him at that very moment.

An alligator splashed suddenly in the water nearby and then there came the soft sound of men moving through the cane on foot. They must have left their mounts some distance away so that they would not give their presence away to anyone in the clearing. He reckoned they were less than fifty yards from the edge of the clearing, working their way along the trail.

For a moment he debated whether to warn the two men in the lean-to, then decided against it. He would be better able to take care of this if the men coming along the trail figured that everyone here was asleep. Carefully, he eased the guns from their holsters, crouched down in the shadows and waited. After a time, as his eyes grew accustomed to the pitch darkness, he was able to make out where the tall canes grew high on the far edge of the clearing, where the trail ran into it. He judged that the men would enter there. At the moment it was impossible to estimate how many there were in this bunch, but from the sound they were making, he guessed perhaps half a dozen.

Dan listened to the sounds carefully. He placed the men just beyond the surrounding cane, then heard a low murmur as someone gave an order. Swinging a little, Dan followed the sounds, knew that the men were fanning out a little, to come in on the lean-to from three directions. His prying eyes made out the three shadows that cut into the clearing and began to creep towards the lean-to from the cane. There were some others in the cane itself, Dan knew that if they decided to remain there it would make things difficult for him. He could not deal with these three men and hope to keep his eye on the canebrake too.

'All right, you two. Out of there!' called one of the men in a harsh tone. His voice sharpened as he went on quickly. 'Drop that gun or I'll kill you.'

There was silence for a moment, then Dan saw the old man and the boy being thrust out of the lean-to, into the wet clearing. There was more movement in the cane and two other men stepped through.

'Three horses out yonder,' said one of them in a thin tone. 'Where's the sleeper in this outfit?'

'Right here.' Dan stepped out into

the clearing, saw the outlaws stiffen abruptly at the sound of his voice. One man whirled, going down into a crouch, his gun coming up to cover Dan. The clearing rang with the single gunshot and the man toppled back, dropping limply to the ground as the bullet hit him.

'Anybody else want to make their play?'

The four outlaws stood staring down at their dead companion. One of them swore harshly under his breath, lifted his head to stare across the clearing at Dan. 'So there was a man hiding out in the cane,' he said slowly. He did not take his gaze away from Dan, watching him, eyes like a snake's in his shadowed face. 'I guess we made a mistake.'

'That's right. Now shuck your gunbelts — hurry!' Dan took a couple of paces forward, levelling the guns so that they covered the men standing in a small group in front of the lean-to. He said to the boy: 'Take their gunbelts when they drop 'em. Then we'll decide what to do with these killers.'

'You're talking big now, mister,' snarled the man who had spoken first, the leader of the group. 'But you won't be so big when the boss gets to you.'

'Get those gunbelts shucked or none of you will live to see that day,' Dan snapped.

With a curse, the men dropped their gunbelts, all except the leader, who seemed to hesitate, fumbling with the buckle of his belt as the boy moved forward to pick up the guns. Then, quickly, not moving towards the boy as Dan had expected him to, the leader swung on the older man, grabbing him around the waist, pulling him in front of him as a shield, at the same time, drawing his gun.

'All right, mister,' he snarled. 'Now back up or the old man gets it in the back and if you think I'm fooling, just try it and see.'

Dan felt a little thrill go through him as he searched the eyes of the man holding the gun. The boy had stopped picking up the guns, was standing in the middle of the clearing, looking about him uncertainly as if unsure of what to do at this sudden turn of events.

'Drop that gun, stranger.'

Dan held back a second, wanting to gauge the other. The click of the pistol hammer told him that the outlaw meant business, that he would shoot the man down in cold blood, without a second thought. There was nothing he could do. Slowly, he lowered his arm and it was at that moment, that the boy made his move. With a sudden yell he straightened up, whirled one of the gunbelts around his head. The heavy buckle caught the outlaw's hand and he yelled suddenly as the gun exploded. The bullet ploughed into the canebrake and the man fell sideways, clutching at his wrist. One of the other bandits shouted something, tried to close with the boy, fell clutching at his stomach as Dan fired, triggering the gun again as one of the other outlaws tried to make a move. The man clawed at his shoulder, his breath sighing out between clenched teeth.

The remaining outlaw stood with his hands lifted. Dan moved forward, eyes alert for any further trouble, but for the time being, all of the fight seemed to have been knocked out of the men.

The old man stepped forward, eyed Dan with a look of approval. 'Mister,' he said. 'that was some of the slickest work I've seen, slipping off into the canebrake like that. How'd you know they was here?'

'Heard them moving around in the cane,' said Dan shortly. 'They must've left their mounts some ways so as not to make much sound. I figured I didn't have a chance so long as I was in the lean-to, but if I was out here in the cane, I might be able to take them by surprise.'

'Well, it sure worked out that way,' Matt nodded. 'What do we do with them now?'

'I figure there's a lot they might be able to tell me about Tollinson's movements and any other men he has along the Trace.'

The man who had been hit in the shoulder lay by the side of the cane. He groaned and tried to sit up, mouthing curses at Dan as the other bent beside him.

'You working for Tollinson?' Dan said harshly.

'My shoulder,' muttered the other, his eyes sullen. 'It's burning like hell. Do something for it, can't you?'

'I asked you a question.'

'I don't know who you're talking about. I've never heard of anybody called Tollinson.'

'You're lying.' A chopping blow to the side of the other's face grazed along the man's cheek and he fell on to his side, yelling hoarsely as pain lanced through his body. When he managed to get back upright, Dan went on: 'I'm not fooling, mister. Tollinson doesn't operate the whole length of the Natchez Trace alone. There's somebody else and I want to know who it is.'

The man remained stubbornly silent. Matt came forward, stood beside Dan, looking down at the man. 'You reckon he knows something about the rest of the gang?' he asked.

'I figure so.' Dan straightened up, turned towards the other two men still on their feet. Cal had a rifle levelled on them and he knew there was no further need for action as far as they were concerned. The boy caught his glance, for he said casually: 'I can handle these two, mister.'

'Doesn't look as though any of them intend to talk.' Dan said slowly.

'That's easily remedied.' Matt edged towards the man with the injured shoulder. 'I can make them tell you anything you want to know. Spent some time with the Mingoes. They have their own ways of making stubborn folk talk. Don't reckon it would be hard to loosen this fella's tongue.'

Dan noticed the expression that gusted over the outlaw's face, nodded his head. 'Go ahead,' he said harshly.

'The way I figure it, Tollinson heads one of these syndicates bent on taking over this stretch of the frontier. I reckon he has some men in Natchez too, watching this end of the trail.' Deliberately he turned away and moved towards the lean-to, as the old man took a thin-bladed knife from his belt, thrust it into the glowing centre of the fire in the middle of the clearing.

The man on the ground watched the proceedings with a look of terror on his swarthy features. He yelled suddenly: 'You keep that crazy old coot away from me. I told you I don't know anything about this *hombre* Tollinson. Me and the boys just figured we might be able to get some grub and maybe a few dollars from you, that's all. We don't — '

'Save your breath,' Dan told him tersely. 'Either you talk now, or Matt here will see to it that you do. You've got a choice.'

Matt waited for a few moments, then drew the knife from the fire and moved over to the outlaw. Dan kept his eyes on the other two men, knowing that if there was to be any trouble it would come from them. He did not doubt that Matt would be able to make this man talk. He had heard a little of the torture methods used by some of the Indian tribes who had lived here before they had been pushed back west by the relentless onward march of the white men.

Seeing the hot blade of the knife moving towards his face, the man cringed back, striving to draw his head as far back as it would go, a look of terror washing over his features. His eyes were open wide, staring up at the riverman who leaned over him, lips drawn back in a thin snarl.

'You still going to say nothing?' asked Matt softly, his tone ominous.

'I tell you I don't know anything. I — ' The man screamed as the point of the blade pricked his throat just below the chin, drawing blood.

Matt said in that same soft voice,

'Better think again before I push this blade a little deeper.'

The man swallowed, his Adam's apple bobbing up and down nervously in his throat. The muscles of his neck were corded under the skin. For a moment, his gaze flicked towards his two companions, standing a few yards away in the darkness. Then he nodded his head as much as he dared, staring across at Dan.

'All right, I'll talk, but keep that knife away from me.'

'That's better,' Dan nodded. He made a gesture with his hand. 'You're working for Tollinson, aren't you?'

The outlaw nodded. He put one hand up to his shoulder where the blood was seeping through into the cloth of his jacket. 'He's got a place in Natchez-under-the-Hill, little saloon off the front street, the *Mississippi Trail*. He goes there every now and again to see Vannier, who runs the place for him. That's how they can watch every part of the Trace.'

Dan nodded. Already, a plan was beginning to form in his mind. If he could tie Tollinson in with this notorious outlaw, Vannier, action would have to be taken against the rancher. There was a hefty price on Vannier's head, dead or alive. This was the kind of evidence he needed, but it was not going to be easy to get at. Natchez-under-the-Hill was the rendezvous for all of the lawless scum along the whole length of the Mississippi. A man went in there at his own risk.

# 4

## The Warning

Andrew Tollinson walked into the small lobby of the hotel, went over to the desk and woke the sleepy clerk lying in the chair behind it. The man opened his eyes briefly, closed them again, then came sharply upright as the rancher caught at his shirt, bunching it in his clenched fist, giving him a sharp pull that hauled him roughly off his seat.

'You seen Aaron Lewis?' he asked sharply.

'Lewis. Why — yes, Mr Tollinson. He came in half an hour ago. I think he's in the dining room.'

A glinting expression showed on the rancher's face as he released his hold on the clerk, thrusting the other backward so that he stumbled heavily over the chair. 'I'll find him,' he said ominously. He stalked across the lobby and into the small dining room, looked about him with a growing impatience, then spotted the lawyer seated at one of the tables in the far corner of the room, and went over to him, sitting uninvited in the empty chair.

Aaron glanced up, then his eyes narrowed as he saw who it was, his face tightening a little. He said with a sharp edge to his voice. 'Sit down, Mr Tollinson. You look as though you've got something on your mind.'

'That's right, Lewis.' Tollinson glanced round as the waiter appeared at his elbow. 'Bring me a whisky,' he said harshly.

When the other had gone, he leaned forward and said in a low undertone: 'I think it's time you and I came to an understanding, Lewis. I know you haven't been actively engaged in trying to fight me, but that girl friend of yours has. She still prints these things about me in that newspaper of hers even though I've warned her what could happen.'

'What do you think I can do about that?' asked Lewis. He chewed on a mouthful of food, washed it down with a gulp of coffee. Inwardly, he felt uneasy, wondering what was in the other man's mind. Tollinson, he knew, rarely did anything unless he had a very good reason, and he had something in his mind when he had come into town to seek him out like this.

'I think you can do a lot,' muttered the other. He paused as the waiter brought his drink, sipped it slowly, eyeing Lewis over the rim of the glass. 'You know her better than most. Warn her off this or I'll have to do things my way.'

'Your way?' Lewis lifted his head sharply. There was a little tremor in his mind at the other's tone. 'What do you mean by that, Tollinson?'

'I think you know damned well what I mean. This *hombre* Carson has been giving me plenty of trouble lately. I reckon I've been too soft-hearted with both him and Jennifer King. I've already taken steps to see that Carson doesn't trouble me much longer. But Jennifer King is a different matter. Either she stops what she's doing, or I'll have to make sure she does.'

Lewis shrugged, trying to appear outwardly calm. Inwardly, his heart was thumping madly and his blood was leaping throughout his veins to its wild rhythm. A filming of cold sweat came to his forehead as he stared intently at the other.

'You trying to tell me that you killed Jennifer's father?' he said tightly, forcing evenness into his tone.

'I'm telling you nothing, lawyer,' Tollinson snapped. 'I'm just warning you of the consequences if your girl friend doesn't stop acting against me.'

'You lay a finger on her and I'll — '

'You'll what?' sneered the other. He leaned forward over the table. 'I've only got to lift my finger and fifty men will ride into New Orleans. If I give the word, a bullet could find you in the dark, no matter where you try to hide. Remember that in case you start getting some ideas.'

Tollinson finished his drink and got heavily to his feet. He stood for a moment, knuckles resting on the edge of the table. 'You going to have a talk with her, tell her what I said?'

Lewis swallowed. Then he nodded his head jerkily. 'I'll tell her,' he said thickly.

'You'd better. I've got too much at stake to have a woman stand in my way.'

Turning on his heel, he walked out of the room. Lewis sat quite still at the table as the other vanished from sight. Inwardly, he was trembling, and when he looked down he saw that his hand was shaking a little as it held the cup of coffee. A sudden savage anger went through him as he drained the cup, set it down on the table. He knew with a sick certainty that Tollinson would not hesitate to kill Jennifer if she continued her campaign against him. But Jennifer was a headstrong girl and he doubted his ability to get her to change her mind. She already felt strongly that Tollinson had been the murderer of her father and she meant to even the score with him no matter what it cost her.

He thought the whole thing over carefully as he picked a cigar from his pocket, lighting it and drawing the tobacco smoke deep into his lungs. Perhaps if this man Carson had not ridden into New Orleans, all of this might not have happened. Carson was the man who had somehow provided Jennifer with the courage she needed to go on with this wild campaign against Tollinson. Even now, when he, Lewis, felt certain that the rancher was her father's killer, he doubted if there was anything that could be done without plunging this country around New Orleans into a blood-bath. And would anyone help in the fight against Tollinson? Certainly not the settlers. Even though they were being robbed and killed by these outlaws they would never band together to fight. And the same went for the rivermen who were forced to use the Trace to get back to Kentucky.

He found Jennifer in the newspaper office. The old man who helped set up the type was busy in one corner near the new press. The girl glanced up in surprise as he pushed open the door and stepped inside. Her smile faded a little as she noticed the look of concern on his face.

She watched him now out of extremely grave eyes. 'You look troubled, Aaron,' she said.

'I've just had another talk with Tollinson,' he said, closing the door after throwing a quick glance up and down the street. 'He came to warn me that something might happen to you unless you stop printing these things about him. Seems Carson is causing him plenty of trouble along the Trace and he's going to stop him permanently. He'll do the same to you, Jennifer, if you don't stop. He's too big a man for a few of us to try to fight.'

'You're going soft, Aaron,' said the girl quietly. Her voice held a firm ring to it. 'Why,' she asked, 'is it that everyone is afraid of him?'

He studied the question and he tried to answer it, and could not. Shrugging, he stared down at his hand as if hoping to find the answer there. 'I'm not a gunman, Jennifer. I don't want any part in killing and murder, even if people think that it's for the best.' He stopped, unsettled by his inner feelings, brought back again by his own fear.

She said: 'Tollinson is an outlaw. Such men don't deserve to live among a decent society. If we want to make anything of this country, then we shall have to fight to rid it of men like him. I'm fighting in the only way I know how. So is Dan Carson. We may be going about it in two different ways, but at least we're fighting.'

'Then you don't intend to stop?' asked Aaron tonelessly. 'In spite of his warning?'

'No, I don't.' For a moment, there was an expression almost of loathing in her eyes as she stared at him in the dim-lit room. 'I know my father would have wanted me to do this if he'd been alive. Tollinson and his men can kill me, as they did him, but some day, people are going to realize the sort of menace which exists here, and when they do, it will mean the end for Tollinson and his kind.'

★ ★ ★

Natchez was a sprawling town, perched on a wide bluff which overlooked the stretching flatness of the muddy Mississippi. Here, the riverboats came, bringing supplies for the wealthy plantation owners, for the stores and saloons, bringing also the gamblers and the vice kings. It was the end of the trail as far as wagons were concerned and the wide streets seemed to be full of them.

Dan kept his gaze moving as he rode

through the wide street. He had learned enough from the outlaws they had taken along the Trace to know where he was going and what he could expect. Whether he could worm his way into Vannier's confidence, long enough to learn anything of value, he did not know. It would be extremely risky, but that was a chance he had to take. He did not know what Tollinson might be doing at that moment, back in New Orleans, or even if the other was still there. He thought he knew now where Tollinson got his gunmen. The other would ride the Trace as far as Natchez, get the men he needed and take them back on one of the riverboats. That was obviously where he had been when Dan had bumped into him.

He did not ride on into the town itself, but instead took the steep down-grade path which led to the edge of the town, down to Natchez-under-the-Hill, the hide-out for all of the thieves and outlaws who roamed the waterfront of the Mississippi. Here, leading off the narrow street, were the saloons and gambling dens which went to make up this hell town. Ten minutes later, he found the Mississippi Trail, a small saloon halfway along the street. Tying his mount to the hitching rail, he went inside, ducking his head low to pass under the lintel of the door. The atmosphere inside the saloon was full of blue smoke and the smell of sweat and stale whisky. Whale-oil lamps hung from the beams, and in their yellow light, he was able to make out the men who sat around the tables there, drinking and gambling, while here and there, dark-haired Spanish girls passed among them. A girl was singing a haunting, lilting song as he entered and he paused to listen to it, leaning his shoulders against one of the pillars, rolling himself a smoke. His mouth and throat felt dry and parched and he did not need the smoke, but a cigarette could be used for several purposes and here it would give him the chance to study the situation, to size things up, before he made any move.

Slowly, he let his gaze wander around the faces of the men in the room. He recognized their kind at once. All bore the stamp of the outlaw and the gambler. Pushing himself away from the wooden pillar, he went over to the bar at the far end of the saloon, ordered a rye whiskey, drank it slowly. He watched the men at one of the tables and began to feel tight inside. He would have to walk with very great care here if he wanted to stay alive. The moment any of these men discovered who he was and why he was there, it would mean the end of him. There was only one thing to his advantage at the moment. No one would expect him to walk into this den of thieves like this, even if they knew he was in Natchez. He had left the three outlaws to the tender mercies of the two rivermen, felt sure they would not allow them to get away to warn Tollinson of what had happened.

The barkeep moved back as Dan

lifted a finger, poured him another drink. Dan jerked a hand towards one of the tables nearby. 'Can anybody join in the game?' he asked.

'Reckon so.' The other glanced along the bar. 'Buck,' he called loudly. 'Somebody here wants to try his luck.'

A man at the table looked up, let his gaze roam over Dan. Then he gave a brusque nod. 'Sit down, mister,' he said thinly.

Dan lowered himself into a chair. The man who had spoken was a whiplash of a man dressed entirely in black, with a gold ring in one ear, dark-skinned with hard eyes. He had a cheroot between his teeth and when he struck a match and lifted it, the yellow flare shone on the planes of his face, highlighting them, gaunt and high-boned.

French, Spanish, American and possibly Indian and Negro blood seemed to be in his veins and his close-eyed gaze missed little. 'You a stranger here in Natchez?' he asked. His tone seemed pleasant enough, but it held a note of something more than mere curiosity.

'That's right,' Dan nodded. 'Just headed in from New Orleans.' He placed his stakes in the middle of the table, glanced at the cards he held. Two kings and little else.

'You here on business?'

'That's right. Business for Tollinson.' He spoke as casually as he could, knowing that this was probably the moment which was crucial.

He saw the dark man's brows lift just a shade, then the impassive look was back. The other nodded. 'You work for Andrew Tollinson?' It was more of a question than a statement of fact.

'Been working for him for three months now,' Dan said. 'But this is the first time I've been to Natchez. There was some slight trouble back on the Trace, but it's been dealt with now.'

Smoke had turned the room blue and in the distance, he was able to pick out the faint click of roulette wheels as the other patrons crowded into the saloon. Dan was surprised to see how many men there were.

'Know where Vannier is?'

The other gave him a bright-sharp stare. 'You got business with him as well?' he asked. He called Dan's hand a moment later without waiting for him to answer, a faint smile on his lips as he had won and he scooped the chips towards him.

Dan nodded. 'Tollinson wants to know how things are at this end. He sent me over to find out. Seems he reckons there may be trouble soon.'

'And if he's right, what sort of trouble?'

'He figures the state governor has been hearing stories about what's happening along the Trace. There may be soldiers sent.'

'The Governor doesn't have enough soldiers for that,' said the other with conviction. 'There are too many raids being carried out by Indians on the settlements west of here. He'll have to take care of them before he can spare any men for us.' The other grinned.

'But if you have to see Vannier, he's through in the back room. Reckon you'll soon get to know this place if you work for Tollinson for any length of time.' He jerked a thumb in the direction of the door at the side of the bar. As Dan made to push his chair back, he said a trifle more sharply. 'No point in going through right now. He's busy. Better have a few more hands.'

Dan forced himself to relax. He wondered whether he had convinced the other of his genuineness as one of Tollinson's men. It was impossible to tell from the other's face what he was thinking as he dealt the cards round again.

The game continued for another hour, with Dan losing steadily to the others. As he played, he let his gaze move around the room, taking in everything. He reckoned that he was safe for the time being so long as none of Tollinson's men who knew him, arrived. He played with only half of his attention on the cards, was glad when the game finally came to an end. The dark-skinned man finished his drink, then scraped back his chair and motioned to Dan. 'I'll take you through to Vannier now,' he said.

The room at the rear of the building was more tastefully furnished than the saloon itself. Dan looked about him in surprise, then let all of his attention go to the man who sat there. He reckoned that Vannier was about fifty years old, tall, hard-featured. He looked hale and hearty but the long scar down one cheek, which drew up that side of his face slightly, marred his otherwise good looks, giving him a curiously leering expression, pulling up one side of his mouth into a perpetual smile.

'One of Tollinson's men,' said Dan's companion. 'Says he has business with you.'

For a moment, Dan was scared as the cold, pale-blue eyes flicked over him, seeming to look through him, although he knew that the other's gaze had missed nothing. 'You say you're from Tollinson?'

'That's right.' Dan forced himself to speak casually. 'He's been having trouble along the Trace. There's been a lot of talk against him in New Orleans and he's going to stop it.'

'So?' The other's eyes grew still and Dan could see suspicion beginning to flare in their depths.

'He sent me to find out how things were at this end. He wants to be sure that everything is all right before he makes any new move.' As he spoke, Dan gave a quick glance towards the man at his back. 'This is news for you,' he went on meaningly.

'Velasquez can be trusted,' Vannier said harshly. 'If you have anything more to say you can say it in front of him. Tollinson knows and trusts him.'

'Then I guess it's all right,' Dan nodded. 'There's trouble brewing for Tollinson in New Orleans. People are getting stirred up ever since he killed that fella King. Now his daughter is printing things about him that he doesn't like. He figures that if she goes on like this, sooner or later, the townsfolk will start putting things together.'

'Why doesn't he stop her like he did her father?' There was an utter callousness in the other's tone which sent a little chill through Dan's mind. He began to wonder just how safe he really was here.

'He doesn't want to do that unless he's forced. Two killings in a row would be too much.'

'And the trouble along the Trace?'

'Some *hombre* by the name of Carson.' Dan tried to keep all emotion from his voice. 'Helping the whipsawers.'

'I've heard of that.' Vannier nodded his head slowly. His look was enigmatic as he got slowly to his feet. His eyes were like flint arrowheads. 'Does he want me to take care of Carson?'

'Tollinson reckons he's hiding out in the canebrake fifteen miles from here on the trail back to New Orleans. If you take enough men, you ought to be able to finish him for good. He's probably got some of the whipsawers with him, so you may have a fight on your hands.'

Vannier grinned and the twist of his lips added a fierceness to his features as he said softly: 'We'll take care of him.' His gaze came back to Dan and he caressed his upper lip. 'You meaning to stay in Natchez?'

'For a couple of days. Then I'll be riding back to tell Tollinson you'll take care of everything.'

'Better tread carefully around Natchez-under-the-Hill,' said the other with a hint of warning in his tone. 'Even if you are one of Tollinson's men, there are plenty of men in town who would slit your throat for the money you're carrying and think nothing of it.'

'I'll be careful,' Dan said. He eased the pistols in his belt a little, then stepped towards the door. 'When will you move out?'

The other's stare hardened. Suspicion was in his eyes again. Then he threw back his head and uttered a harsh laugh. 'When I've got my men together,' he said. 'No cause for you to worry any more about this. You've delivered your message. I'll do the rest.'

Dan shrugged. 'Suits me,' he said shortly. He rubbed his chin. 'Reckon I'll get myself a bed for the night. It's been a long ride on the Trace.'

Going out, he moved through the saloon, the blue smoke swirling about him. The roulette wheels were still clicking and more and more patrons were continuing to stream into the saloon. The people here seemed to allow their enjoyment to go on well into the night and the early hours of the morning, he reflected. He moved out into the street, drew the cool, moist air that flowed from the river, deep into his lungs. So far, he seemed to be safe. How much of his story Vannier had believed, he wasn't sure.

But if the other did ride out with

some of his men as he had said, Dan considered it might be possible for him to ride out to some of the settlers, get some of them to ride back with him along the Trace and take Vannier and his men by surprise. It was a long shot, he reasoned, but if it worked, they might be able to take Vannier back. He wasn't thinking so much of the money which had been offered for the outlaw leader, as the fact that it might then be possible to get Vannier to talk, particularly if it could be made to seem that Tollinson had betrayed him.

A riot of half-formed thoughts and ideas were bubbling inside his mind as he stepped up into the saddle. In the darkness, he did not notice the man who had just ridden up to the saloon and who now stood in the shadows on the side of the doorway, lighting a cigarette, watching him closely from under a wide-brimmed hat.

After he had ridden off down the narrow, muddy street, the other slipped into the saloon and made his way quickly to the rear room.

Vannier looked up as the man entered, frowning his annoyance. He said sharply, as he got to his feet: 'What are you doing here, Mason?'

'Never mind about that, Vannier,' muttered the other harshly. 'That *hombre* who just came out. Any idea what he was doing here?'

'He came from Tollinson. Seems there's trouble ready to break. I've to take some of the boys and take care of it myself.'

Mason's eyes narrowed to mere slits. 'You telling me that he came in here and said he was from Tollinson?'

'That's right.' Surprise showed on the other's face. 'What's on your mind? You trying to tell me Tollinson didn't send him?'

'I'll say he didn't. That was Dan Carson. I thought I recognized him the minute he stepped out of the saloon. He tried to kill me some time back in New Orleans when he shot down the foreman.'

Vannier's lips twisted into a hard line. He fingered the scar on his cheek unconsciously. Then he seemed to control himself. He had his own temper but he did not allow it to take control of his emotions. 'I see.' A wide grin touched his lips, a vicious expression and there was a bright gleam in his deep-set eyes.

'You want me to follow him and take care of him?' asked Mason. His hand dropped suggestively to his gun butt.

'No. I'll do this my way. Are you sure that he didn't see you?'

'Sure I am,' said the other positively.

'Good. Then we'll let him go on thinking that he's tricked us. He'll be back here soon. I want him alive. A quick death is too good for him.'

★   ★   ★

The bed had been hard and lumpy and Dan had slept badly during the night. The sound of revelry had died only an hour or so before dawn and the town

181

had settled down to a brief period of silence before the new day dawned, the pale grey light settling on the broad stretch of the river. As the dawn light filtered in through the half-open window of his room, he lay flat on his back, his hands locked behind his neck, staring up at the peeling ceiling over his head. The sounds of the town had broken down into isolated shards of noise now with the occasional hooting of a riverboat tied up at the levee not far away.

He never seemed to be very far from the river these days, he reflected tiredly. First New Orleans and now here. He tried to think ahead, but there were so many imponderables that he knew any plans he tried to make might be doomed to failure right from the beginning. If only he knew what was happening in New Orleans. He was feeling uneasy about that girl. She had made a more lasting impression on him than he had thought possible. She had the courage that most of the men there seemed to lack. But that courage could be the undoing of her. Tollinson would not stand for her getting in his way much longer. And the fact that she was a woman would not weigh with the other at all. She would be merely someone else trying to finish him and he would stop her by any means in his power.

He got up a while later, ate a quick breakfast, then went out into the street. The sun was just coming up, glinting on the river that flowed serenely by. There were four riverboats tied up at the levee, disgorging their cargo, or taking more on for the last lap to New Orleans.

Here there were rows of dingy warehouses that fronted the levee and he moved in a silence that was broken only by the sound of his feet on the red brick and limestone which would soon absorb the heat of the day. The boats which lay alongside the levee were of every different kind he could possibly imagine. There were the big, palatial boats for the Mississippi trade, carrying passengers along the broad river. Others, flat-bottomed and sternwheeled with short upper decks that offered little resistance to the sweeping winds of the open plains where they did most of their trade.

Even now, so early in the morning, the levee was bustling with activity. It seemed to be the only part of the town that was alive now. Roustabouts were working, toting the bales of cotton and the other goods on board, moving slowly up and down the narrow planks which had been laid from the decks to the quay. Dan squatted himself crosslegged and watched, feeling the growing warmth of the sun soak into his body. He found himself wondering about Vannier. More and more, the thought of the other man troubled him. Vannier had not got to where he was now by being a fool and accepting every man who came to him, on trust. The other might be trying to check up on him in some way and if he succeeded, it could mean trouble, although it was unlikely that there was anyone in Natchez who knew him or who could recognize him.

He heard steps behind him and turned to see his aquaintance of the previous night striding resolutely towards him. The other still wore his black frock coat and his dark eyes rested on Dan with a seeming indifference; but he said: 'You're to come with me. Vannier wants to see you.'

Dan's first curdling thought was that somehow, they had found out about him, then he put the idea from his mind with an effort. If that had been the case, he reckoned, they would have killed him by now, not giving him the chance to fight back or cause them more trouble. Sucking in a deep gust of air, he got to his feet and fell into step beside the other. They moved swiftly along the dingy streets with the warehouses lifting on either side of them. Here there were bleak alleyways and between-building spaces which promised trouble but he allowed nothing to show on his face.

'You know what it is Vannier wants to talk about?'

'You'll find that out when you meet him,' said the other. He did not seem as talkative now as he had been on the previous time they had met.

Deep down inside, Dan did not trust this man, or Vannier, nor the message which had been brought to him, but at the moment there was nothing he could do but comply with it. Whatever happened, these men must not be made suspicious while he was still in the town. He glanced about him as they made their way along dark alleys where the sunlight never seemed to penetrate. The faint, moist wind from the river assailed his nostrils, something he was not used to. This town, and particularly this part of it, down near the river, seemed to live in its own atmosphere of evil.

At the door of the small saloon, he paused, stood for a moment glancing about him. The other took his arm. 'Vannier's waiting,' he said silkily. 'We'd better go in and see what he wants.'

'Sure.' Dan forced a quick nod of his head. The feel of danger was in him, but he followed the other through the swing doors, into the cool dimness of the saloon. The tables were unoccupied now. A swamper was brushing the floor with a slow, mechanical movement, not even bothering to look up as they entered and made their way to the door at the back of the room.

The man pushed it open, stood on one side for Dan to enter, then moved in after him, closing the door behind him. Vannier looked up as they went inside, eyed Dan briefly. 'You're sure that Tollinson wants me to ride out after this *hombre*, Carson?' he said softly.

'That's what I said. I told you last night that — '

'I know what you told me last night.' A slow smile creased the other's jaws and there was a smouldering fire at the back of his pale eyes.

Moisture came out on the palms of Dan's hands, but he forced himself to refrain from rubbing them on his shirt. He knew that both of these men were watching him closely, guessed that something had gone wrong although he couldn't figure what it was. He didn't like the look of this at all, and a little thrill ran through his nerves.

'Then if you know, why are you asking all of these questions again?'

Before the other could speak, the door behind Dan opened again with a faint creak. He did not turn, although he felt the cool draught of air swirl about him for a moment, knew that someone else had come into the room.

A voice that sounded vaguely familiar said: 'Hello, Carson. I always figured we might meet again.'

He turned his head slowly, found himself glancing at one of the men who had been in the saloon in New Orleans when he had been forced to kill a man, Tollinson's foreman. This was also one of those men who had been in the group trying to hang that settler.

'You got nothing to say, Carson?' said Vannier harshly. He came forward and stood in front of Dan. 'That was a nice try, but unfortunately for you it didn't come off. I reckon that Tollinson is going to be mighty pleased to hear that we've finished you. But that was the message you brought, wasn't it?' He threw his head back and laughed and the sound of it caused Dan to shiver inwardly.

'Carson, you've given me plenty of reason to shoot you down here and now, just where you stand. But I've been thinking this over since Mason rode in and I reckon that Tollinson wouldn't like it if you went as easy as that. I've got something else in store for you, my friend.'

'Could be that you're figuring on shooting me in the back,' Dan said slowly. He gained a feeling of satisfaction from the red flush that crept into the other's face. Then the other seemed to gain control of himself again.

He shook his head slowly, grinned viciously. 'I reckon we've got something in store for you that will please Tollinson mightily.' His grin widened.

Dan cursed him and at the same moment, lunged forward. His head caught the outlaw full in the chest, sending him sprawling back, arms flailing, caught by surprise at the suddenness of the attack. As he teetered on his feet, Dan sent over a short, jabbing left that landed on the man's chin before he thudded on to his back in the middle of the room.

He turned then, knowing that the two men behind him would be moving in swiftly. One hand went for the gun at his belt but a sudden sharp blow on his wrist forced him to drop it. He saw Mason's teeth bared, the cruel, bright look in his eyes as he came in, with the half-breed close behind. Dan ducked under Mason's wild, swinging blow, hammered a couple of return blows to the other's ribs, felt the man give way with a rasping grunt as the wind was driven from his lungs by the force of the blows.

But before he could swing to meet the other man, he glimpsed the upraised gun as the man brought it swinging down at his head. There was no time to duck or move away. The gun barrel cracked viciously against the side of his skull and Dan seemed to go rolling off down a bottomless slope with bright stars flashing all around him.

★　★　★

There was the sensation of drowning and for one wild moment, with his numbed mind playing tricks on him, he thought he was back in the muddy waters of the Mississippi after being dropped overboard from the paddle steamer by Andrew Tollinson. He gasped wildly, tried to move his arms and legs, then opened his eyes. Water was dripping from his hair on to his face, blinding him, running down his cheeks and dripping from his chin. He shook his throbbing head as if trying to make the pain go away by simply moving, then winced, screwing up his eyes against the harsh, vivid glare of sunlight that fell full on them.

A man stood over him, legs braced well apart, a man who was little more than a pain-blurred shadow, with the sun at the back of him, so that it was impossible to make out his features. Sucking air down into his lungs, he tried to focus his wavering vision on the other, struggling to recognize the man. His mind seemed fogged and dazed and he found it difficult to remember anything. Then, gradually, memory returned. He recalled that last meeting with Vannier and the gun butt which had cracked down on his skull, knocking him out.

'So you've finally come around.' Mason squatted down beside him, the dripping bucket held in his right hand.

A further spasm lanced through his head and he tried to lift his hands to clutch it and it was then that he discovered he was bound hand and foot. Narrowing his eyes, he forced himself to look about him. It was difficult for him to orientate himself and his body seemed to be swaying gently from side to side with a curiously sickening motion. He guessed the blow on the head had left him light-headed and he would feel better once he was able to sit up.

'That was some stunt you tried to pull with Vannier,' said Mason casually. 'I reckon if I hadn't happened along when I did, you might have pulled it off. Pity, because it means the end of the trail for you.'

'I wouldn't be too sure of that,' Dan said through tightly clenched teeth.

'No?' There was a mocking note in the other's voice. 'We got all this figured out, Vannier and me. You got any idea where we are?'

'No.' Dan licked his lips. He knew he was out in the open for he could see the clear, cloudless blue of the bright, sunlit heavens over his head. But even that didn't help to tell him where they were.

'We're headed for the far side of the Mississippi,' said the other, still grinning. 'Plenty of swamp there and once your body is tossed into the bayou, the alligators will soon make short work of you. Nobody will be any the wiser about what happened to you.'

So that was what they had in store for him. In spite of the tight grip he had on his mind, Dan felt the sweat begin to ooze from his body, filming his forehead. It was a diabolically clever thing to do, getting rid of him without any trace. Like Mason said, nobody would know what had happened to him; he would simply vanish from the face of the earth and in time, nobody would ask any more questions about him.

Mason moved a short distance away and Dan managed to roll over on to his side. He could see a little more of his surroundings now, saw that he was on the deck of a flatboat. There was only

Mason there, no sign of any of the others. Evidently, they had decided that with his guns taken away and tied hand and foot, he would present no problem for one man. It was impossible for him to see the water, but in the distance, just over the bow of the boat, he could make out the low trees which stretched along the far bank of the river. Somewhere in there, Mason would push him over the side of the boat, possibly on to one of the low mudbanks, leaving him there for the first 'gator that happened along. The thought sent a little shiver coursing through his veins. Keeping an eye on the man in the bow of the boat, he drew up his legs as far as he could, twisting them behind him, struggling to reach the knots of the ropes that bound his feet with his fingers. Mason evidently considered him to be helpless, for he concentrated on watching the river ahead, not once turning to glance behind him. Pain laced through Dan's leg and shoulder muscles as he strove to reach the knots. Unable to move his fingers more than a few inches, feeling the sweat break out afresh on his forehead, and on the palms of his hands, making them slippery with moisture, he finally managed to catch hold of the knots, tugging at them savagely with all of the strength in his pliable fingers.

At any moment, Mason might decide to turn and check on him, but now they were working their way off the main stream, into the swampy banks and tiny tributaries of the Mississippi. The trees leaned down to touch the water here, long fronds brushing over the deck of the boat as they drifted among the trunks that lifted from the shallow, muddy water. Mason had picked up the long paddle now and was steering the flatboat expertly among the trees, occasionally ducking his head as a low branch passed overhead.

Slowly, painfully slowly, Dan managed to loosen the knots. His fingers became numb with the pressure he was forced to exert and the clawing fingers of cramp lanced through the muscles of his legs and thighs, knotting them into hard balls of flesh, forcing him to bite his lower lip, until the blood came, to prevent himself from crying out. He felt sore and bruised all over and the throbbing pain in his head was growing somehow worse, as if a thousand tiny hammers were beating at his brain.

'You've not got much longer,' Mason called without turning his head. 'This is going to give me a great deal of satisfaction to dump you into the swamp here. I figure I might stay around for a while, just to see that the 'gators don't leave you alone too long.'

Dan said nothing. He felt the bonds that tied his legs loosen, slackening as he succeeded in untying the knots. Very carefully, he stretched his legs out once more, thereby relieving the spasm of cramp in them. The sweat felt cold on his forehead. In front of him, Mason laid down the paddle, got unsteadily to his feet as the flatboat began to rock a little. Very carefully, he made his way back, lips drawn over his teeth in an animal-like snarl of triumph.

'Better say any prayers right now,' he said hoarsely. 'Once them alligators scent you, it'll be the finish.' He paused and looked about him into the dim trees of the bayou. Vaguely, Dan heard a faint splash, then another, guessed what it was.

'Here they come now,' said Mason throatily. An alligator bellowed hollowly in the green depths of the swamp. 'They sound hungry.'

'You don't think you'll get away with this, do you, Mason?' Dan said thinly.

'That oughtn't to worry you.' The other turned and stared down at him, took a step forward. 'In a few minutes you'll be dead. With you out of the way, I figure we can handle Lewis and the girl back in New Orleans. You were different to them. You knew how to handle a gun and I reckon Tollinson made a big mistake when he tried to kill you on that boat. Maybe if he'd left you alone, you'd have been no trouble. Not that anything can change that now.' He bent to get his hands under Dan's body, to roll him over the side of the flatboat.

It was at that moment that Dan moved, knowing that it would be now or never as he drew back his legs, then kicked high, aiming for Mason's belly. He caught the look of sheer surprise on the outlaw's face as the realization came to him that the ropes around his legs were no longer tied. Mason tried to twist out of the way of Dan's lashing feet. He was half turned when they hit him in the midriff, knocking him sideways. Before he could regain his balance, one hand clawing desperately for the gun in his belt, Dan kicked at his ankles, twisted one foot behind the outlaw's leg, kicking savagely with the other. Mason gave a harsh, high-pitched scream as his legs went from under him. For a moment he teetered on one foot, arms flailing swiftly as he strove to regain his balance. He was perilously close to the edge of the boat and he seemed to realize his danger all at once, for the look on his face changed from one of stunned surprise to one of real, abject terror. Then he was gone, falling back over the boat which rocked dangerously for a moment as his boots slipped on the deck. Dan heard the splash as Mason hit the water and swung himself up on to his side, getting his feet under him. Even though his arms were still tied at his back, the rope cutting into his flesh, he managed to balance himself, staring down into the brown, muddy water at the spot where Mason had gone under. A series of ripples spread out over the smooth surface of the swamp with the flatboat drifting slowly on it.

For a long moment, there was no sign of the other. Then the outlaw came bobbing up to the surface a few yards away, arms striking at the water in fear as he tried to swim after the boat. Glancing beyond the struggling man, Dan saw something which sent a chill of fear through him. The long, slender shapes that came knifing through the water with a deceptive speed, sending out scarcely any ripples at all, the ugly, warted snouts just showing above the water, were less than ten yards from Mason now as he tried to swim, his wet clothing dragging him down. He tried to touch bottom, went under again with a wild yell, came up spluttering and cursing, knowing his danger but unable to do anything about it.

Clenching his teeth, Dan felt the sweat break out on him anew as the faintly-seen tracks arrowed in on the doomed man. Even though he knew that Mason had planned this for him, he still felt a surge of helpless tension in him. The end came swiftly and, bound as he was, there was nothing he could possibly do to avert it. There was a rush of water, a blur of foam splashed high by Mason's beating hands as he tried to fight off his attackers. Then the outlaw was dragged under, a shrill scream bursting from him. The flatboat rocked and swayed as the ripples caught it. Sickened by the sight, Dan forced himself to turn away, lowered himself carefully on to the deck of the boat. If he didn't move carefully, he might tilt the flatboat so much that it would pitch him into the swamp.

Shaking his throbbing head, he forced himself to think clearly. Mason was dead, but he was still not out of trouble. The first thing he had to do was free his hands. That took him half an hour of painful, patient working, rubbing the ropes against the sharp-edged metal of the stern, taking most of the skin from his wrists, before he was free. He sat for several moments, rubbing his chafed wrists to bring back the circulation, then grimly, he went forward, picked up the paddle which Mason had discarded, and began to work his way back towards the river.

Once Mason failed to return, Vannier would have the suspicion that something had gone wrong and he would be able to call on plenty of men in Natchez to hunt him down. The sooner he got out of here and headed back for New Orleans, the better. For the time being, he would have to abandon any hope of drawing Vannier out of Natchez into the open when it might be possible to destroy him.

He felt groggy, head aching dully as he worked his way among the trees. Every tiny channel seemed alike to him in the later afternoon sunlight and the glare of the sunshine off the rippling water made his head ache worse as it shone in his eyes. He tried vainly to recall which way they had entered the bayou, knowing how easy it would be to get hopelessly lost in this wilderness of trees and swamp. The smell of the bayou was strong in his nostrils, the smell of damp, rotting vegetation, sweet and cloying. Like the smell of death, he reflected, dwelling for a moment on the way in which Mason had died. The thought evoked a little tremor in his mind, disturbing him afresh. He turned the boat into a wider channel, now in more of a hurry than he had been before. The silence of the bayou seemed to be a signal of things to come, an emptiness and suppressed quiet that ate like acid at his nerves.

The sun was setting by the time he finally came out of the vast swamp. In front of him, the river lay wide and silent. He realized at once that he must have worked his way some miles downriver in his attempt to get free of the all-embracing arms of the bayou, for there was no sign of Natchez, or of the levee where the riverboats had been tied up that morning. He paddled the boat over the river, fighting the broad, onrushing current with the last ounce of his strength, keeping his eyes alert for trouble, but not expecting any. He felt sore and bruised all over, aching in every limb. There was dried blood encrusted on his wrists where the ropes had cut deep into his skin and he vowed that Vannier would pay for this in like coin the moment his first opportunity of getting the other alone came.

The Tollinson outfit sure wanted to make sure he didn't stay alive to bother them any more, he reflected inwardly, edging the boat towards the far bank. It seemed that they had never cottoned on to the idea that anyone might come along into this territory to start bucking against them. So far, they had had a clear field, with Tollinson able to buy up the small ranches and homesteads along the Trace at a nominal price, or take them for nothing at all depending on his whim. Now he was determined he would rub them raw until they hollered for mercy and until Tollinson and Vannier were either dead or behind bars awaiting trial. He felt sure that there would be plenty of charges preferred against them if it ever came to that.

# 5

## Gun Breed

Aaron Lewis and Jennifer King drew rein in a small grove of cottonwood and pine that overlooked a narrow stream, halting there to water their mounts. In the cool sunlight that filtered down through the branches overhead, the girl's face was in half shadow and Aaron turned in his saddle to watch her as she looked through the trees, to where the land lifted in a rising sweep of green a mile or so along the trail.

Her lips were clear and ample against the tan of her face and there was a clear depth in her eyes which made her seem gay and yet serious at the same time. She felt his gaze on her for she turned her head, the long hair falling about her shoulders. For a moment there she had seemed a lost spirit, he thought, her mind far away, and a little nagging suspicion tugged at the corner of his mind.

'Jenny,' he said softly. 'What goes on in that pretty head of yours? You seem to be so far away these past few days.'

'Nothing,' she said quietly. 'I'm just wondering what Tollinson intends to do. He's going to do something and this waiting for it to happen isn't easy on the nerves.'

'Why don't you forget about Tollinson and this whole business? If you marry me, there'll be no need for you to keep up this work on the newspaper and then there'll be no danger from Tollinson or the others. We could even go away from New Orleans altogether. There's nothing keeping me tied here. I could get a job as a lawyer in almost any town in the country and once away from this town, you could forget the misery that has happened here in time.'

'Is that all you have on your mind, Aaron?' she asked quietly. 'Trying to forget that there's trouble in this world?

It won't do us any good to try to run away from it. These people come here because they're trying to start up a new life in a new country. They've saved and they've sacrificed to buy the land and no sooner do they get here than Tollinson starts moving in, robbing and threatening, killing them if they don't get out.'

'Nothing you or I can do will alter that, Jenny,' said the other harshly. 'I've tried to explain this to you so many times that it seems to me you just don't want to listen. You're blind and stubborn just like your father.'

For a moment there was anger at the back of her eyes and she sat tall and straight in the saddle. Then she pushed it away and studied him over a thoughtful interval. 'Aaron,' she said finally, 'I'm going to do something my father failed to do. I'm going to see that Tollinson gets everything he deserves and nobody is going to stop me. You're very blunt when you feel that you don't have to be charming to me. Maybe you think that without your help I can't do anything.'

'I don't think you can fight Tollinson alone and there's no one in New Orleans who will risk his neck to help you.'

'Not even you, Aaron?' Her glance ran over his face and a sudden flicker of expression came to her eyes and lips, making her features seem a trifle harder than before. She was obviously trying to judge him, trying to get behind his thought and words. 'You knew my father, you knew the principles he stood for, those he would never abandon, no matter what happened, what threats were made against him. He believed that people were entitled to the same protection of the law, that a man had a right to live in peace. He hated those who tried to move in and drive people off their land which they had obtained honestly. He could hate, but you'll find that I can hate harder and stronger than he ever could. He was a simple man, with simple ideals who believed that most people were as good as he was. I've seen the badness and the evil that lives in men and I know I can fight it as he never could. You'll never be certain with me, Aaron.'

The other slid from the saddle. Standing in the rough grass, he looked up at her and said sharply, seeing her in a different light. 'You seem to be taking a very realistic view of everything all of a sudden, Jenny. Is this your way of saying that you don't want to marry me? Because I won't throw everything away trying to fight the inevitable?'

'Aaron,' she said gently, 'I can almost read your mind. You know as well as I do that Tollinson was the man who killed my father. You do a lot of things so well, but you don't have the moral courage to stand up for what you know to be right. You're a lawyer and you must know when a thing is right and when it's wrong. And it's always been the case, down through history, that if a thing is worth having, it's worth fighting for.'

'Then why don't you let the settlers fight for their rights, without you getting involved in it? It's none of your affair.'

'It's everybody's affair,' retorted the girl hotly. A faint rosy flush had spread up into her cheeks and her eyes were brighter than before. 'There's a man who's fighting now and — '

'You're talking about this man Carson.' Aaron's lips tightened into a hard, thin line. He nodded his head as though in some kind of secret understanding. 'I thought it might be that. He's not for you, Jenny. He's just another brush-jumper, riding ahead of the law. Sooner or later it will catch up with him if Tollinson and his men don't get him first. What sort of a life do you think you'd possibly have with a man like that? He'll take the first trail over the hill as soon as trouble shows. Maybe that's why he came here, running from something in his past. When this is finished, if he's still alive, he'll start looking over his shoulder again, ready to be on the move once more, and so it will go on for him, never ending.'

'You never did have a very good opinion of him, did you?'

Aaron gave a quick shake of his head. 'I had him figured out as that kind of man the minute I saw him, standing over that dead foreman with a smoking gun in his fist. First impressions are usually right where I'm concerned.'

'Well in this case, I think you were wrong. He told me that Tollinson had tried to kill him on the riverboat coming down to New Orleans, that the other had offered him a job with his outfit and when he had refused, Tollinson tried to silence him in case he did any talking once he got here.'

'Naturally, he would tell you something like that,' remarked Aaron drily. 'You didn't expect him to tell you the truth, did you?'

Jennifer looked at him directly. 'I know he was telling me the truth,' she said firmly.

'You've only known him for a little while. How could you possibly know whether or not he was telling the truth about a thing like that?'

'There are things you instinctively know about people,' she said quietly, squarely. 'Just as you formed your first opinion of him and — '

She broke off quickly at a sudden sound. There was the crackle of twigs snapping in the underbrush and a moment later, a party of riders came out into the clearing beside the narrow stream.

Andrew Tollinson headed his men as he rode forward. He paused a few feet away, smiling sarcastically. Aaron tensed and his hand dropped to his side where he kept the small pistol. But his fingers came away again as if they had touched something white-hot as one of the men levelled a rifle at him over the saddlehorn of his mount.

'Just keep your hands where we can see them,' said Tollinson thinly. He gigged his horse forward, reached out quickly and grasped the reins of the girl's mount. Jennifer tried to use her whip, slashing angrily at him, striving to hit the leering face in front of her, but Tollinson easily evaded the quirt, leaning back in his saddle as he did so, grinning a trifle viciously. 'I warned you what would happen if you didn't listen to sense,' he said thinly. 'Seems you want to get yourself killed.'

'Just like my father, you mean,' snapped the girl, her eyes blazing. 'You were the one who killed him and then made it look like an accident.'

'Of course,' Tollinson nodded. He did not look disturbed by her statement. 'But there's nothing you can do about it now. I don't mean you to go on attacking me in that newspaper of yours. You've written your last article on Andrew Tollinson.'

'Now see here, Tollinson,' began Aaron. He moved closer to the other, then stopped as the rancher rasped: 'Stay where you are, lawyer. You've interfered in my affairs as well. Even

214

though you haven't been as open about it as the girl, you're still a menace to me.'

Aaron clenched his hands into tight fists, lips thinned in anger. 'You harm Jennifer and I'll — '

'Now don't get nervy, lawyer,' said the man with the rifle. He chuckled thinly. 'We don't want to have to shoot you down right here in front of the lady. That wouldn't be nice.'

'Quiet, Hill,' said Tollinson. 'I'll give the orders when there's to be any shooting.' He glanced sideways at the girl. 'You're coming with us. Maybe then we can stop this *hombre* Carson from creating hell along the Trace as far as my boys are concerned.'

Jennifer smiled up at him insolently. 'I'm glad to hear that someone has you worried.' she said harshly.

'He won't be doing it for long,' muttered Tollinson ominously. 'I've already taken steps to see that he's taken care of.'

'Better take care he doesn't get you

first,' retorted Jennifer King quietly.

'If he tries, you won't be here to see it.' There was a veiled threat in the rancher's voice. 'You'll be riding with us.'

'Where are you taking her?' Aaron made another move towards the other, came up sharp as the barrel of the rifle was lowered a little to follow his movement. A little thrill ran along his nerves. He knew there was nothing he could do to stop these men, that even if he tried, it could only end in his death and that would not help the girl in the slightest. He clamped his lips tightly together, teeth clenched in his head so that the muscles of his jaw lumped under the skin.

Tollinson smiled triumphantly. 'We're taking her along the Trace,' he said softly, 'to a place where neither you nor Carson will be able to find her. Maybe we'll let her go if Carson rides in and gives himself up. Maybe . . . '

Tollinson's throaty laughter mingled with the girl's faint cry. Desperately, she touched spurs to her horse in an attempt to break free of Tollinson's tight, restraining grasp on the reins. Aaron had the fear that in her anger and desperation, she might make a try for the small gun she carried and that could mean the end for both of them. Harshly, he said: 'Ease off, Jennifer. These men won't get away with this. If they try to kidnap you, it will be the last straw as far as the citizens of New Orleans are concerned and Tollinson here knows that he'll have a posse on his tail before he's gone a day's ride into the Trace.'

The smile remained fixed on the rancher's face. He shook his head slowly. 'If there's nobody left to talk to the men in town, they won't bother to come looking for anybody,' he said threateningly.

'Why you — ' began Aaron. 'Now I know the stripe of coyote you really are, Tollinson. I should have figured you out long ago.'

'Pity you didn't,' sneered the other.

His eyes narrowed, yet he still held the crooked smile. He glanced at his companions. 'Let's get this over with. No sense in hanging around here any longer.'

Aaron tensed himself. He licked his dry lips and looked from one man to another, not sure of what was coming next. He knew his position was hopeless. Sooner or later, one of these men would pull a trigger and blast him into eternity. He gritted his teeth, wondered how he could have been so stupid as to allow himself to get into this position. He tried to appear outwardly calm as Tollinson grated: 'Better get back up on your horse, mister lawyer, and ride on out of here. Try anything funny and you'll get a bullet in you.'

'I hear you, Tollinson,' Aaron said tightly. 'I suppose you want me to turn my back so you can shoot me down from behind like you've done most of the other men you've killed.'

Tollinson shook his head soberly.

'Now you're asking for me to change my mind, Aaron. Better do like I say, get on your horse and ride on out of here, any direction you want to go except back to New Orleans. You might cause me more trouble back there.'

'I'll see you hanged for this, Tollinson,' said the girl harshly. She whirled in the saddle.

'I ain't losing any sleep over that possibility,' said the other. He did not take his gaze off Aaron. 'Now are you going to do like I say or do I have to gun you down right here, lawyer?'

Heart thumping in his chest, Aaron Lewis edged towards his horse, calmed it with one hand, then put his boot into the stirrup, bracing himself inwardly for the bullet he felt sure would be on its way at any moment to smash into his spine. He was swinging himself up into the saddle, when he heard the girl give a faint scream. Almost, he managed to turn, then flopped forward on to his face over the horse's back as the rifle shot cracked out and something hit him heavy and hard below his shoulder, knocking him forward over the saddle. He was only briefly aware of the horse bucking under him, leaping forward, splashing through the shallow water of the stream, before the blackness came, welling up around him and shutting out the world.

*  *  *

Dan rode through a stretch of heavy cane, then crossed a short bare bench and reached more timber, the trail climbing again into low foothills. He had deliberately avoided the main trail through the cane since pulling out of Natchez three days earlier. The horse he had taken from in front of one of the saloons while its owner was drinking inside. He felt a wry, grim amusement in him as he thought about it. It seemed he was wanted for so many things now that stealing another horse wouldn't add up to much.

Half an hour later, he came to the summit of this narrow, winding trail and here he stopped, looking down into a narrow ravine that dipped through the trees, with tall rocky walls lifting sheer on either side. He was nearing New Orleans now, reckoned he could not have been more than five miles from the outskirts of the town and there might be trouble waiting for him along this stretch of the trail, especially if Vannier had somehow got word through to Tollinson.

Putting his mount downgrade, he withdrew into his thoughts as he rode. So many things had happened since he had ridden into New Orleans that he found it difficult to straighten out his ideas. There was going to be a bad end to this fighting between Tollinson and the settlers and the feeling was growing in his mind that he could well find himself in the middle of it, although the quarrel there was nothing to do with him. He had only this score to settle with Tollinson and Vannier.

The canyon was at least forty feet deep and the bottom was rocky and difficult for the horse to negotiate but he made it finally, rode out into more open country with tiny springs gushing down the side of the foothills, bubbling over the smooth stones, glinting in the late afternoon sunlight. By degrees, the trail widened, grew more open, with plenty of space between the trees. This was the pleasant stretch of country that lay just to the west of New Orleans and he guessed that the Tollinson spread ought to be somewhere in this area. He rode slowly now as the thought crossed his mind, not wanting to run into any of Tollinson's men.

Shadows streamed out far from the trees now that the sun was lowering behind him, his own shadow running before him. The spicy air that lay motionless among the trees was beginning to shimmer a little as coolness came into it and he could feel it on his heated face, cool and refreshing. There was a falls nearby. He could just hear the thunder of it as it splashed down the side of the hill and the misty dampness of its closeness hung heavy in the air.

Then, above the sound of the waterfall, he heard something else, a sound that jerked his head up sharply, eyes narrowed, searching the trail around him as he recognized the steady thrumming of a solitary horse. It was coming nearer, but he judged that the rider was not on the same trail as he was, was probably moving parallel to him, lower down towards the distant valley.

One of Tollinson's men? It was possible and he drew his mount deeper into the scrub, eyes alert, trying to judge where the other was. There were several vague, faint echoes, reflected back from the steep walls of rock close by, muffling the sound sufficiently to make it impossible to guess accurately where the man was. Down below him, perhaps a quarter of a mile away, there was an opening between the trees and he could just see the narrow scar of the other trail through it. The other rider was down there somewhere if only he could see him. Dan felt tightness grow in him. He had the feeling that things had been happening here that he ought to know about before he went much further.

A dimly-seen form drifted out of a bushy hollow, moved swiftly across the open stretch of ground and vanished into the trees which blocked Dan's view on the other side.

But Dan had seen enough to realize that there was something far wrong down there. Whoever the rider had been, he had either been seriously wounded or killed, for he had been lying caught in the saddle across the back of the running horse, not sitting upright.

He guided his own mount off the rim of the hill trail, put it down a short wrinkle in the ground, then over a thorny stretch of bush, feeling the spiny branches rip at his legs as he rode through them. Halfway down the rockstrewn slope, he lost sight of the man below once again, but he had seen enough to know almost exactly where he was. Here and there, the ground was studded by gaunt trees which bordered the valley trail and he cut the slope at an angle, racing on to the distant trail behind the fleeing horse. Already, it was half a mile away, kicking up dust.

It was too far away for him to recognize the man who lay sprawled over the saddle and he told himself that it could be one of Tollinson's men for all he knew. There might have been a gun battle hereabouts with some men killed or wounded on both sides, although who would dare to stand up to Tollinson and his band of hired killers, was beyond his comprehension. Unless Jennifer King had somehow got word to the Governor and he had been forced to act at long last to protect the settlers.

Some ten minutes later, he reached the trail, gave his horse its head and slowly began to overhaul the other horse. Brush abounded in thick clumps at intervals along the trail. Here and there, a shallow stream ran across it, the crystal clear water splashing up around his horse's hooves as he put it across. Finally, at a sharp bend in the trail, he drew alongside the horse, managed to reach down for the bridle, and hauled it up. It halted at last, lathered and trembling.

'Steady, boy,' he said softly. 'No one's going to hurt you.'

He slipped from the saddle once he was satisfied that the horse was settled, moved around and lifted the man's head, let a gasp of surprise escape from his lips as he recognized the other.

'Aaron Lewis,' he said aloud. Gently, he lifted the lawyer from the saddle and stretched him out on the rough grass that grew at the edge of the trail. The other's jacket was soaked with blood at the back and he turned him over on to his stomach, cutting through the cloth with the sharp blade of his knife. He soon discovered the ugly wound just below the right shoulder blade. Fortunately the bullet had entered obliquely, and he reckoned it had missed the heart by a goodly piece and had probably also missed the lung. But the lawyer had lost a great deal of blood and he would have to be got to a doctor as quickly as possible if he was to have any chance of survival at all.

Making a wad with his handkerchief, he stuffed it firmly against the wound and bound it with a strip from the other's shirt. The lawyer groaned deep in his throat although he still seemed to be unconscious. Hoisting him back across the saddle, he was forced to tie him down. Then he turned the horses and headed back along the trail to New Orleans as quickly as he could.

Lewis regained consciousness several times on the trail back into town, tried to mutter something but the words seemed muffled and indistinct and it was impossible for Dan to make any of them out, and the lawyer lapsed back into unconsciousness again within seconds.

The street was almost empty as Dan rode down it, leading the other horse and its unconscious burden. A man rode by in a buckboard, gave him a sharp, though cursory, glance, his shoulders hunched forward against the growing evening coolness. Another man dismounted from his horse in front of the nearby saloon, went inside through the batwing doors without looking round.

Reining in front of the doctor's place, Dan slipped from the saddle, pulled Aaron Lewis's unconscious body from the saddle and carried him to the door, hammering loudly on it with his knuckles.

There was no answer for a long moment, then he heard the shuffle of feet on the other side of the door, a chain rattled and a lock snapped back. The door opened and the grey-whiskered man stood peering out at him. The other gave a faint gasp of surprise as he caught sight of Dan, then he stood on one side, motioning him to enter.

'It's Aaron Lewis,' Dan said through his teeth. He carried the young lawyer into the room which the other pointed out to him at the end of the passage, lowered him on to a couch, then straightened up with a grunt. 'He must've been shot in the back somewhere along the trail. I spotted his horse with him lying across the saddle, headed away from town and managed to stop it. He's been hurt bad, I'm afraid.'

'I warned him about this some time ago,' said the other, in a dry tone. 'But he wouldn't listen. Reckon he was too tangled with King's daughter to worry about the possible consequences.'

'You figure that Tollinson did it?'

'Could be,' said the other, his tone non-committal. 'But I doubt if you'll ever prove it unless he comes round.' He examined the wound in the lawyer's back, sucking in his cheeks as he did so.

'He's luckier than most,' he went on finally, 'the bullet must have caught him at an angle. It's gone up towards the shoulder blade, possibly nicking the lung, although I don't think so. I'll have to probe for it and I'll need help in case he comes round. Think you could hold him while I dig for this piece of lead?'

'Go ahead,' Dan said quietly. 'I'll keep a tight hold on him if he comes to.'

The other went into the adjoining room. He came back five minutes later with a tray of boiling water and some instruments in it. Dan gently eased the wounded man over on to his stomach under the doctor's directions, taking care not to move him more than was actually necessary. Lewis groaned once as the pain in his body reached down even into his unconsciousness.

Placing his hands on the man's shoulders, Dan held them there while the other got to work, probing in the wound for the offending piece of metal. It had lodged deep against the bone and there was sweat standing out on the other's face long before he finally located it, easing it out gently with the slender, metal forceps. At last, after what seemed an eternity, during which Lewis twisted on the couch several times as pain bit deep into him, the piece of lead was out and the doctor dropped it with a metallic thud on to the table nearby.

'That's it,' he said softly. 'Now if he hasn't lost too much blood and there are no complications setting in, I reckon he'll live. He's got a tough constitution which will stand him in good stead now.'

Dan nodded. 'I reckon I'll go along and tell Miss King,' he said firmly. 'She'll probably want to see him.'

'Better tell the marshal too while you're about it,' suggested the other.

Dan paused at that, then he shook his head. 'Not just yet,' he said quietly. 'If I'm right, and Tollinson is at the back of this, the less Marshal Thorpe knows about it, the better. He's more likely than not in cahoots with Tollinson and I don't want any word of this getting through to him until I'm good and ready.'

The doctor looked surprised, then shrugged. 'You know what you're doing, I suppose,' he said. 'But he's sure to find out sooner or later and if he discovers you've been keeping evidence from him, there'll be hell to pay.'

'I'll take that chance.' Dan moved to the door. Outside, it was getting dark as the reds and golds in the west began to fade swiftly, with the night swooping in from the east, blotting out all of the colours except the deep blues and purples, bringing the bright stars with it.

Dan walked swiftly along the slatted boardwalk. A few of the people abroad gave him a sideways glance, then hurried by, evidently recognizing him, but not wanting to be recognized by him, knowing instinctively that he meant trouble.

At the newspaper office, Dan paused,

rapped loudly on the door. There was no light inside the room and although he pressed his face close to the glass, he could see no one inside. Troubled, he moved away, convinced that there was something wrong. At this time of the night, Jennifer King was always there, getting everything set up for the next day's edition.

He was on the point of moving away, when he heard the faint call from the end of the dark alley nearby. Cautiously, suspecting a trap, he moved forward, his hand hovering close to his belt. The man who stood there in the shadows, moved towards him and a moment later, he recognized the oldster who helped in the office.

'I thought I knew you,' said the other in a hoarse whisper. 'I've been waiting here for Miss Jennifer to show up. She should have been here an hour ago but there's been no sign of her.'

'Do you know where she went?' Dan asked quickly. He felt the tension beginning to rise in him, riding him, but he forced himself to relax.

'She went riding with Aaron Lewis shortly after noon. They took the trail west. I saw them go myself and that was the last I saw of either of them.'

'With Aaron Lewis. You're sure of that?' The feeling of uneasiness suddenly crystallised in Dan's mind. If this was the case, then where was the girl? Had whoever shot Lewis, also killed the girl? He realized that he was clenching his fists tightly by his sides, forced them to open.

'Course I'm sure,' said the other indignantly. 'Do you think I'm simple-minded? I saw them ride out. Miss Jennifer said she would be back in time to set up the type this evening, but it's late now. We'll never get it done in time now, even if she does come.'

'I've got a feeling she won't turn up,' said Dan softly. He kneaded the muscles at the back of his neck with his fingers, trying to think things out logically. There was only one chance now of finding out what had happened to the girl. If anyone knew, it would be Lewis. Somehow, he had to get the other to talk even if he had been shot in the back. The longer he waited, the more start these attackers had, always assuming that the girl had not been killed out of hand, as had obviously been intended with Lewis.

Dan came back swiftly along the street, alert for trouble. There was no light in the marshal's office as he passed and no sound from inside. Better not to go looking for the lawman anyway, he decided. There were big things at stake here and if Tollinson cracked the whip, he did not doubt which way Thorpe would jump. It was the cattlemen's money and votes which had put him where he was and unless he played their game, turned a blind eye whenever a settler was burned out or murdered, he would not last for long in town.

For a moment, he paused in the shadows opposite the doctor's house. The yellow light from the lamp still shone through the window, spilling out on to the boardwalk and a man strode by, just visible in the darkness as the beam of light fell slantwise over his face. As Dan watched, another light came on in one of the other windows. Going noiselessly forward, he stood quiet on the boardwalk near the window. The sound of voices reached him as he stood there, one hard and demanding, the other firm and more quiet. He could not make out much of what the doctor was saying, but it was not difficult to recognize Thorpe's gruff voice as he said loudly: 'Now look here, Doc, I don't want to sound officious, but you know my position in town and if there's been a shooting here, then I want to get to the bottom of it. You said yourself that the bullet just glanced off his shoulder blade without doing him too much internal damage. All I want to do is ask him a few questions and then I'll be on my way and look into this. I need to know where the shooting occurred and who found him and brought him back into town.'

Moving quickly, Dan slipped along the alley to the rear door of the building, found it open, and went noiselessly inside. The rear room was in complete darkness but he managed to feel his way forward, guided to the door by the strip of yellow light that showed under it. Still keyed to danger, guessing why Thorpe had really come, he took one step into the other room, the door opening soundlessly under his hand. Thorpe and the doctor had their backs to him as he entered, oblivious of his presence. Aaron Lewis lay on the long, narrow bunk which had been pulled away from the wall, his shoulder bound up in a broad bandage, eyes closed, only the slow rising and failing on his chest to show that he was still alive.

'He can talk to you all you want in the morning, Marshal,' said the doctor firmly. 'At the moment, I want him to sleep. He needs rest now more than anything. I've done all that I can for him medically, now it's up to nature to help the healing process.'

'Then maybe *you'd* like to tell me how he got here if he was shot on the trail? It's a sure thing he didn't ride that horse here by himself.'

Dan could see the look of indecision showing on the doctor's features. The two men both whirled sharply as he said quietly: 'You seem to want to know a helluva lot, Marshal. Could it be that Tollinson is getting a mite worried in case Aaron lives and tells us what he knows?'

Thorpe's eyes narrowed and his thick bushy brows drew together into a firm, hard line, his forehead puckered. 'Did you bring him in, Carson?' There was a little snap to his tone as he struggled to regain his composure.

'That's right,' Dan replied easily. 'I found him on the trail some miles out. Looked as though some sidewinding coyote had shot him in the back, left him there to die.

'Couldn't have been you by any chance, I suppose?' said the other sharply. 'From what I hear, you sure had a good enough reason for wanting him dead.'

'That's nonsense,' broke in the doctor hastily. He looked from Dan to the marshal and then back again, a look of puzzled bewilderment on his face.

'Is it?' snapped Thorpe. He stared at Dan as he spoke. 'I guess the whole town knows Lewis tried to talk you out of this stupid idea of trying to fight Tollinson and we know that Jenny King has been mighty cool towards him since you rode into New Orleans. Could be that she took a shine to you, leaving him out in the cold.'

Dan drew in the sudden surge of anger that threatened to rise up and overwhelm him. He recognized that Thorpe was only trying to rile him and grimly determined not to allow the other to get him angry. He forced a quick grin, shook his head slowly. 'No good trying to throw the blame for this shooting on me, Marshal. That charge just won't stick, and you know it. If those outlaws had done the job properly you might have been able to, but as it is, I reckon Aaron will be able to tell us what happened when he comes round. In the meantime, I figure you'd better get back to your job, collect a posse together and ride out after these trigger-happy killers that Tollinson has got with him. Or maybe Tollinson wouldn't approve of that as he was probably the one who pulled the trigger.'

'Why you young whippersnapper,' said Thorpe through tightly-clenched teeth. He took a quick step forward, his hand dropping swiftly to his side, then he froze and pulled up short as the barrel of Dan's gun lined up on his chest in a blur of motion too swift for the eye to follow.

'Back down, Thorpe,' Dan grated harshly. 'I don't want to have to kill you in cold blood but I will if you force me. If there is anything I hate it's a crooked lawman, hiding behind a badge. You're even worse than these outlaws. At least they show themselves in their true colours.' There was naked scorn in his voice and he could see by the workings of the marshal's face that his words were getting home. 'Now get out of here!' The uneasy fear he felt for Jennifer King's safety coloured Dan's voice.

Thorpe hesitated, then caught the look in the other's eyes and turned quickly on his heel, hurrying out of the room. In the doorway, he paused, said thickly: 'You'll regret this, Carson, I promise you.' Then he was gone before Dan could repeat his threat. He heard the other's footsteps fading into the distance along the boardwalk outside.

'Well,' said the doctor, 'what did you find out?' He spoke over his shoulder as he went about the room, pulling down the window shades, then locked the street door.

'Plenty,' Dan told him, 'and all of it bad. Jennifer King rode out with Aaron here shortly after noon. Nobody seems to have seen her since.'

The other stood by the bed staring

down at the injured lawyer, his face troubled. 'Then whoever shot Aaron has either killed Jenny or taken her away with them,' he said dully.

'I'm afraid so. That's why, in spite of what you told Thorpe, we have to bring Aaron round now, get him to tell us what happened. I'm going after them once I can find out where they've taken her, always assuming that she's still alive.' He felt the tightness grow in him.

The other looked doubtful, noticed the expression on Dan's face, said quietly and softly: 'All right, I'll see what I can do.'

Dan waited with a growing impatience. The man on the bed groaned finally, then his eyes flicked open. For a long moment he stared up at them with no sign of recognition in his eyes. Then his gaze fastened on Dan's face and a faint grin spread over his lips.

'So you came back,' he said in a hoarse, low tone, muscles of his neck cording as he fought to get the words out. He drew back his lips suddenly as a spasm of pain lanced through his shoulder. 'What happened? How did I get here?'

'I found you on the trail, lying across your horse,' Dan told him quickly. 'We want to know what happened out there and where Jennifer King is. She was with you when the shooting occurred, wasn't she?'

'Jennifer.' For a moment the other repeated the word as if trying to remember who she was, then he nodded and tried to sit up in the bed, but the doctor pushed him back, gently but firmly, holding his hands on the other's arms to keep him down. 'Just lie still,' he said firmly, 'and you'll be all right. You haven't got to excite yourself. You lost a good deal of blood before Dan got you here. Now try to think, tell us all you know.'

'You going after them?' muttered Aaron in a thin whisper. His eyes rested on Dan's face.

'If you tell me who they were and what happened.'

'It was Tollinson and a bunch of his gunmen. They jumped us on the trail, took Jenny away with them. Tollinson said that nobody would come looking for her if there was no one left alive to say what had happened. I guess he figured I was dead when that hireling shot me in the back as I was climbing into the saddle.'

'Then Jenny is still alive?'

'So far as I know.' Aaron swallowed and tried to nod. Sweat stood out in a thin, glistening film on his face and forehead. 'He said they were taking her along the Trace to someplace where nobody would find her. When you gave yourself up, they'd release her. I figure they think that if you're out of the way, she won't be able to cause them too much trouble.'

'And you reckon they'd keep their promise, even if I did give myself up?' Dan said. There was disbelief in his tone. 'But so long as they're only holding her as hostage, there's still a chance.'

'The Trace stretches a long way,' said the doctor quietly. 'Clear to Natchez and Nashville, on into Kentucky. They could have her anywhere. It would take you a year to search every possible hiding place.'

'Mebbe so. But I'm figuring that Tollinson won't want to travel too far with a woman. I reckon he'll have some place between here and Natchez. Besides, he's got a man named Vannier watching the Natchez end of the Trace.'

'Try to get some men to ride out with you,' whispered Aaron. He gripped the bedpost more tightly, knuckles standing out white, as pain went through his body once more. 'Get some of the settlers to go with you. There's a man called Callard. He's a good man with a gun and I know that Tollinson has been threatening him for some time now. He's got friends. They've been talking of banding together for a while now. Maybe this will precipitate them into action where nothing else would.'

# 6

## Vengeance Trail

Dan reached his horse, rode out along the main street and then made a wide circle of the town. The moon had risen, round and yellow in the east, throwing a wide swathe of light over the placid waters of the Big Muddy in the distance. He took the road that led to the north, a solid road of hard-packed dust which would be turned into a stream of mud once the rains came. But at the moment, it was a good trail and he made excellent time as he rode up into timber, heading north, in the direction of Jem Callard's spread. There had been wisdom in what Aaron Lewis had said. If things could only be worked properly, there was a chance they might be able to finish Tollinson once and for all. The rancher would not be expecting a party of settlers to ride down on him at his hiding place somewhere along the Trace. He would consider himself to be absolutely safe, believing he had only one man to take care of, a man who would soon come out of hiding once he learned that the girl had been taken hostage.

He kept on the road, moved up over the brow of a steep rise, now in more of a hurry than he had been. It still wanted another couple of hours to midnight, but he had a long distance to cover and little time to waste. The thought of the girl in Tollinson's hands disturbed him anew and he ran over in his mind all of the places he had ridden through along the Trace to Natchez, trying to pick out any which would serve as a safe hiding place. The trouble was, there were so many suitable spots where a bunch of men could hide out, with little fear of being discovered.

An hour later, when he was some miles up into the hills, he picked out the first rumour of other riders in the night, moving ahead of him. They had evidently taken another trail, unknown to him, which passed over the valley, and they were pushing their mounts at a punishing pace. He reined up and listened intently, striving to pick them out in the moon-washed darkness below him. Then he caught sight of them, a tight-packed bunch, spurring across the plain, heading north. A little sense of awareness caught at his mind, heightening the tension in him. The echo of the riders was a steady abrasion which slowly faded. Touching spurs to his mount, he urged it forward, over the crest of the rise and then down the other side.

Near midnight, he felt the slackness in his mount, knew that it wanted to slow and continue at its own pace, but he forced it on. The sight of those riders heading north had given him the feeling that maybe Tollinson, or the marshal, was one jump ahead of him and there was no time to waste if he was to reach Callard. A little later, with starlight making a vague trembling glow over the surrounding countryside, he crossed the trail and smelled the dust in the air, kicked up by the riders in front of him. Above the gentle sighing of the wind he could just make out the faint tattoo of the horses in the distance and the conviction came to him that it had been Thorpe he had spotted, heading out for Callard's place. Maybe the marshal had figured that Dan would need help if he went out after Tollinson and Callard and the settlers were the only people likely to provide him with this much-needed help. Therefore Thorpe had decided to put a stop to this as soon as possible and he had got his posse together and they were riding out to take Callard and some of the others by surprise.

The feeling of helplessness grew in Dan's mind as he rode. He knew with a sick certainty that he could not hope to catch up with that bunch of men now, before they reached the Callard spread. The dust stayed with him as he rode on, watching the grey-black foreground of the trail as it twisted in front of him, rising and dipping over low hills, always cutting north.

He was more than five miles from Callard's place, riding through a clump of heavy timber when the break of gunfire reached him from dead ahead. He reined his mount sharply, bending forward in the saddle. The sound of shots came and went, with steady volleys interspersed by individual gun-shots. Savagely he dug rowels into the horse's flanks. It responded gallantly, jumping into a dispirited run, shoes striking the ground hard as it plunged out of the timber, into the open again.

The shooting stayed brisk as he drew nearer, then gradually died with only the crack of potted shots following one another at irregular intervals. With perhaps half a mile still to go, he heard the firing die altogether and a moment later, there was the unmistakable sound of a solitary horseman spurring towards him, back along the trail, travelling in a hurry.

Dan reined up, drew in to the side of the trail and waited. He caught sight of the rider while he was still some distance away. As the other drew to within twenty feet of him, Dan edged out into the middle of the trail and laid his gun on the other's chest.

'All right,' he yelled harshly. 'Stop right there.'

The rider reined up hard, his mount pawing at the air. With an effort, he managed to get it under control and a moment later, Marshal Thorpe said harshly: 'Who the devil is that?'

Dan moved forward. He said softly: 'You look as if you're riding from something, Marshal.'

'Carson!' There was an odd edge to the marshal's voice. He lifted the reins, made to kick his mount into a run, to brush past the man in front of him, then paused as Dan said: 'I'll drill you the first wrong move you make, Thorpe. I figured you would be in on something like this. What happened yonder?'

'You're obstructing the law, Carson.' There was a little quaver in the man's voice now. He threw a quick, apprehensive glance over his shoulder as a fresh sound broke out. More riders came along the trail and the look on Thorpe's face changed to one of fear. He shouted: 'Get out of the way, Carson. I'm warning you I'll — '

'You'll stay right there, Thorpe.' Dan looked beyond the other as the riders came up. He recognized Callard in the lead. The settler gave him a bright glance, then said with a crooked grin. 'I see you got him, Carson. He's the only one of the bunch left. Rode out like a scared rabbit.'

'I spotted him and the others heading north a while ago, while I was still in the hills, figured they meant to take you by surprise.'

Callard nodded. There was a grim look on his bluff features. 'We got word they was headed out of town and we laid a little trap of our own for them.

They rode right into it.'

'So that was the shooting I heard a few minutes back.' The other nodded. He eyed Dan curiously. 'Were you on your way out to see me?'

'That's right. I need your help.' While a couple of the men watched the marshal, Dan explained quickly what had happened. When he had finished, Callard said tightly: 'You can count us in on this, Carson. Tollinson and his hired killers have been riding rough-shod over us ever since we came here. I reckon it's time for the showdown. You got any idea where they might be hiding out?'

'Could be anywhere, I reckon.'

Callard rubbed his chin musingly, then turned his head a little and looked directly at Thorpe. 'This *hombre* is usually in Tollinson's confidence,' he said meaningly. 'Could be that he knows a thing or two about it.'

'I don't know anything,' said Thorpe, his jaw slack as the meaning behind the other's words penetrated. 'And believe me, you'll have to answer for this. There's such a thing as law and order and I happen to be the properly elected representative in this town.'

Callard gave a derisive laugh. 'You're not fooling anybody here, Thorpe.' he muttered. 'We all know what you are, Tollinson's puppet.' He gigged his mount, moving closer to the other. Without warning, his fist lashed out, caught the other on the side of the head, sending him reeling sideways in the saddle. Thorpe put up a hand to his face, swung his startled gaze around the men gathered in a tight, menacing bunch about him.

'I reckon you're lying when you say you know nothing of Tollinson's plans, Thorpe,' said Callard. 'Your job is to watch things in town and he would have left you orders where to find him if anything went wrong.'

The expression on the marshal's face told Dan that Callard had hit the truth. Sweat stood out on his forehead and he rubbed at it with the back of his hand.

'You going to talk, or do we have to make you?' Callard lifted his hand again and Thorpe cringed back in the saddle. There was a thin trickle of blood moving down from the corner of his mouth where the first blow had cut his lip. The man was obviously a coward, Dan considered, and he doubted if he would hold out against these men for even as long as that outlaw he had caught on the trail had held out against the whipsawer's Indian methods.

Thorpe shook his head. He must have realized the utter futility of his position but he still seemed to be holding out for some kind of reprieve even though he must have known it must have been hopeless, with the rest of his men killed and no help within miles of this spot.

Callard deliberated, then he lifted one of the guns from its holster, held it carefully in his right hand. Thorpe's eyes widened and his mouth dropped open. Evidently he thought that the settler intended to shoot him out of hand, for he gave a tiny bleat of protest. Then Callard's hand moved, only a short distance this time and the foresight whipped down the marshal's cheek, tearing a bleeding line in the flesh. Thorpe yelled loudly, drew his head back, moaning.

'Yes, sir,' said Callard meanly. He slapped the gun against the open palm of his other hand. 'You sure as hell can be made to howl. But if you were sure enough to come riding out with those men and try to finish us off, you must have been mighty sure of what Tollinson is doing right now. Where is he, Thorpe?'

The marshal groaned, stared down at the smear of blood on the back of his hand where he had wiped it down the side of his face. 'Don't pistol-whip me,' he pleaded.

'Then go ahead and talk. We don't have all night.'

'Tollinson will kill me if he ever finds out.'

'I'll kill you right now if you don't,'

said Callard ominously. He loomed menacingly over the other, eyes narrowed to slits.

'He's got a place halfway between New Orleans and Natchez. It's where he often meets Vannier. They find it easier — and safer — than riding into either town to parley.'

Callard glanced round at Dan, who nodded his head. 'Makes sense, I reckon,' Dan murmured. 'If it's true, I think we should take Thorpe along with us. We can always shoot him if he's been lying.'

'It's the truth, I tell you,' said the other harshly.

'Then you'll lead us there,' Callard said. 'And the first wrong move you make will be your last, I can promise you that. I won't think twice about killing a snake like you.' He leaned forward and plucked the marshal's guns from their holsters and tossed them away into the brush nearby. 'Right. Let's ride.'

★ ★ ★

There was a piece of rough tarp stretched over the mouth of the cave in the rock hillside and the smoke from the fire remained caught by it, filling the air so that it brought tears to Jennifer King's eyes as she sat at the back of the cave, her wrists tied. There were three men seated near the opening, rifles leaning against the rocky wall near them. Now and again, one of them would glance over his shoulder to where she was sitting, then turn away, looking down at the well-thumbed cards in his hand.

She had little idea of where she was, except that it had to be somewhere along the Natchez Trace. The party had brought her here the day before and she had been forced to spend an uncomfortable night lying on a piece of rough sacking which had done little to ease the sharp hardness of the stones. Her body felt bruised and cut and the cord around her wrists had cut into the skin.

She had tried, at first, to ease the knots, unsure of what she could do even if she did succeed in loosening them. Now she no longer tried. Whenever her hands were unbound to enable her to eat the food which one of the men brought to her, she tried to restore the circulation in them, hoping that they would forget to tie her up again, but every time, whenever the plates were taken away, one of the men guarding her would bind her wrists again and she would be forced to endure the agony of chafed and bleeding flesh again as the long hours dragged by.

She wasn't sure what time of the day it was. With the tarp stretched in front of the cave mouth, it was impossible to tell whether it was light or dark outside, or where the sun was in the sky. Tollinson had gone off a couple of hours before, and she had heard him say he was heading for Natchez-under-the-Hill and had caught the name Vannier. She had heard vaguely of this outlaw leader who terrorized the Trace near Natchez and from what little she had heard as the men talked among themselves, she guessed that he and Tollinson were working hand in hand, with Tollinson apparently giving the orders.

She lay back, resting her shoulders against the hard, projecting rock. Her position seemed utterly hopeless. She did not know whether Aaron was dead or alive. The last she had seen of him, he had been lying limply over the saddle, badly wounded, for it had been virtually impossible for that gunman to miss at that distance. There was also the fact that Aaron's mount had been carrying him along the trail away from New Orleans.

She felt a growing sense of defeat in her mind, closed her eyes, trying not to think of what might lie in store for her when Tollinson came back. Hours passed in an eternity of fatigue and pain and she lost all sense of time as she lay there, listening with a part of her mind to the men talking, and occasionally quarrelling among themselves. After a while, she fell into an uneasy doze, her head resting on her arm.

When she woke, she was cold and numb. Moving her legs, stretching them out as straight as she could in front her, she felt the agonizing tingle of returning circulation and it was as if a thousand pins were being thrust into her flesh. Gritting her teeth, she forced herself not to cry out with the pain. It was dark now inside the cave and she guessed that it was night outside. Gradually as her eyes grew accustomed to the darkness, she noticed the pale yellow illumination at the mouth of the cave. Moonlight, she thought after a while. Letting her gaze wander slowly from side to side, she managed to pick out the huddled shapes of the two men now left near the entrance. Both seemed to be asleep and their regular breathing was a soft sound in the night.

Holding her breath, she edged a little to one side where a sharp edge of rock protruded from the rear of the cave. If only she could rub the cord that bound her wrists along it, there might be a chance of cutting the rope and freeing her hands. She did not stop to consider beyond that point but twisted herself with an agonising slowness, taking care not to make any more sound than was necessary. Once, one of the men near the entrance grunted in his sleep and rolled over on to his other side. She froze instantly, her heart jumping, hammering madly, into her throat. The blood pounded incessantly along her veins, throbbing in her temples as she waited. When there was no further movement from the men, she edged forward once more, reached the projection, and lifted her hands, rubbing the rope along the rough, sharp edge of rock. Inevitably, her wrists caught against it as she moved them up and down and within minutes they were raw and bleeding, but she gritted her teeth tightly and persisted, knowing that this might be her only chance to escape. Once she was outside the cave, there was a slim chance she might be able to find one of the horses and ride back in the direction of New Orleans before the men awoke or Tollinson and the rest of the men got back from Natchez.

The minutes dragged. Every so often, she tested the ropes, pulling on them with all of her remaining strength, but they continued to hold. Her arms began to ache intolerably with the strain. The tough fibre of which the ropes had been made yielded only slowly and the gash in her wrists deepened. She was conscious of the moonlight filtering into the cave now, touching the corners with shadow. If either of those two guards woke, they would be bound to see her, she thought tensely.

Now she was forced to rest for longer and more frequent intervals, waiting until the pain in her arms eased a little before beginning again. Gradually, she felt the ropes slackening. She took in a long breath, worked with a renewed fury at the ropes, ignoring the agony in her wrists.

At last, when she thought she could go at the task no longer, she felt them give and fall away from her trembling hands. For a long moment she remained there on her knees scarcely daring to move for fear of waking either of the men. Now she would have to be doubly careful, to slip past the two sleeping guards without wakening either of them. She wondered for a brief moment whether either man would shoot her down if he did wake to find her trying to escape, or whether Tollinson had given orders that she was not to be harmed, only kept there.

Getting to her feet, she swayed for a moment and was forced to hold on to the rock to steady herself. The cave swam around her as the blood rushed, pounding forcefully, to her head. Gradually, she was able to focus her vision and began to edge her way forward, an inch at a time, taking care where she placed her feet, so as not to kick any of the loose rocks which littered the floor of the cave.

She held her breath in her lungs as she drew near to the two sleeping men. One man held his rifle between his arms as he slept. The other's weapon lay propped against the rocky entrance just behind the tarp. She debated whether to try to snatch it and use it to defend herself if she was caught, then decided against such a move.

Pulling aside the tarp, she glanced out. In the bright moonlight, she could make out the rocky incline that led down to the thick canebrake in the distance, perhaps half a mile away. Somewhere in that dense mass of cane lay the Trace. Slowly, she moved out, let the tarp fall back into place. She felt exhausted, but knew that now she was free, she would have to put as much distance between these men and herself before dawn. Then there was that third man somewhere around. She could see no sign of him, but knew that he would not be far away.

She started down the slope, searching with her eyes for the horses, knowing they would have to be somewhere close by. Behind her, there was a sudden movement inside the cave, a hoarse shout of warning as one of the men woke, to find that she was no longer there. Swiftly, she turned to run, knowing that she had no chance so long as she was out in the open, with the moonlight picking her out. The rough stones slipped treacherously under her feet, threatening to send her pitching forward with every step she took. Fear began screaming inside her brain. Throwing a quick look over her shoulder, she saw the tarp being twitched aside and one of the men rushed out, staring about him wildly. The cane was still several yards away and she knew she had no chance now, but something in her compelled her to keep on running even though she knew it was hopeless. Then she stopped as a shadow stepped out of the trees almost directly in front of her and she gave a low scream as she recognized Andrew Tollinson. There were other men behind him, a man with a dark, swarthy face, a thin, tight smile on his lips.

'Were you thinking of going somewhere, Jennifer?' asked Tollinson, his voice too casual, too pleasant. 'I'm sure you'd rather stay here. Out there in the canebrake it would be so easy to get lost and there are alligators in the swamps.'

'You'll pay for this, Tollinson,' Jennifer gasped. 'When Dan Carson hears of this, your life won't be worth a nickel.'

Tollinson gave a grin, but there was no mirth in it. 'Somehow,' he said softly, 'I doubt if Carson will trouble me much longer. If he figured he might get some help from the settlers, he'll find that he's out of luck. I left word with Marshal Thorpe to ride out tonight and take care of them for me. You see, I never leave anything to chance. Even if Carson manages to slip through that net, he won't be able to help you. One man against the men I have with me.'

The man standing behind him spoke up harshly. 'I'm hoping that he does come riding in to try to rescue her. I have a score to settle with Carson. You know that he killed Mason?'

'Yes.' The smile vanished from Tollinson's features as if wiped away by a magic brush. 'He has more lives than a mountain cat, but mark my words, they're almost at an end.' He turned to face the two guards who had come slowly down the slope, carrying their rifles in their hands. His voice lashed them angrily. 'I thought I left you keeping watch over her. What were you doing — sleeping?'

'She must have been as quiet as a cat,' said one of the men shame-facedly.

'Take her back into the cave and tie her up properly this time,' Tollinson ordered harshly. 'And tie her legs this time.'

Jennifer moved back into the cave, with the barrel of the rifle prodding her savagely in the back. Her situation had not been relieved. In fact, it had been made worse by her ill-fated attempt at escape. She knew too, from what

Tollinson had said, that there was very little chance of Dan Carson getting through to help her, even if Aaron were still alive and had been able to tell what had happened. Besides, she did not even know for sure where Dan was. She felt a curiously warm feeling go through her as she thought of him. She had never been affected like this by any man in her life, not even Aaron, and she felt a strange sense of wonderment.

The guard tied a fresh length of rope around her wrists and ankles, pulling it tighter than was necessary to relieve the anger he evidently felt at her. She did not doubt that Tollinson would have his own way of making sure that these men paid for almost letting her escape when they had been detailed to keep watch on her and could guess at the thoughts which were running through the guard's mind at that moment, saw the savage anger in the set of his mouth. The look boded ill for her, she thought, but at the moment she felt so utterly weary and defeated that there was no room for fear or apprehension in her mind.

Tollinson walked over, inspected the bonds, nodded in satisfaction. There was a faintly leering grin on his face as he said harshly. 'I don't think it will be too long before Carson hears what has happened and he'll come riding in, either to give himself up, or in a forlorn attempt to rescue you. Whichever way it is, he's finished.'

'And then you'll kill me in cold blood, I suppose.'

The other pursed his lips, stretching them then into a hard line. 'That all depends on you. If you promise to behave yourself, not to keep poking your nose into things which don't concern you, I might be sufficiently soft-hearted to let you go. Somehow, I doubt if you could do anything to harm me once Carson is out of the way.'

'You made a big mistake when you tried to kill him, didn't you?'

'It's a mistake which I shall remedy in a little while, believe me.'

'Maybe he'll prove too clever for you again.'

'Don't start building up your hopes on that happening,' Tollinson laughed thinly and the sound sent a little shiver coursing along her spine. 'I made one mistake, but I don't intend to make another. That is why I brought Vannier along with me from Natchez. He too has a score to settle with Carson. So you see, he doesn't have any chance at all.'

Jennifer let her gaze drift to the other man, standing against the wall of the cave, his eyes resting on her. The look she saw in them increased the uneasy sensation of apprehensive fear in her mind. Here, she thought, was a man who was even worse than Tollinson. The face was cruel, the eyes bleak and without any emotion in them, like the empty eyes of a snake, mesmerizing and frightening. He smiled as he saw her watching him, but there was no mirth in the smile and it was merely a twitching of his lips, something which did not affect the rest of his features. The knife in his hand flashed a little as he turned it over and over in his fingers.

'I'll post a couple of men to watch the trail from both directions,' said Tollinson suddenly, seeming to pull himself together with a visible effort.

★　★　★

Dan sat still on the saddle in the courtyard of the small-holding high in the hills, feeling the impatience grow in him until he could scarcely contain it. After they had got Thorpe, he had been all for riding on west to the Trace and catching up with Tollinson wherever he might be, before the other had a chance to draw any more men to him than he had already. But Callard had maintained that to have any chance at all, they needed every man they could get and had insisted, possibly rightly, that they should visit every settler in the neighbourhood of the hills, rounding them all up, getting them to ride with them on this last showdown. If they did not succeed, then there would be nothing left for them here anyway, but if they did, if they managed to crush Tollinson and his men once and for all, it would mean that the settlers and anyone else who came to buy land here would be able to live in peace.

Thorpe sat slumped in his saddle a few feet away. All of the fight seemed to have gone out of him now, he looked a defeated man, the lines of worry clearly visible on his face in the flooding moonlight.

'I don't know why you're worrying, Thorpe,' Dan told him. 'All you have to do is lead us to where Tollinson is hiding and leave the rest to us. At least you're probably going to get out of this with a whole skin which is more than can be said for a heap of other men.'

'You don't stand a chance of finishing Tollinson,' said the other, his tone listless. 'He can call on twice as many men as you can get together and apart from that, he'll probably have Vannier and some of his men with him, just to make sure of you.'

Dan shook his head. 'Somehow, I don't think he will. He'll be so damned sure that you succeeded in killing off most of the settlers tonight that he won't think of us taking as many men as this with us.'

Thorpe lapsed into a sullen silence. Evidently he had been thinking along those lines too. Dan watched the other's features with a growing alertness. He saw the other draw a sharp breath. Then he became aware of Dan's probing glance and made an effort to hide his feelings.

Callard came riding across the courtyard, his mount kicking up little spurts of dry dust. 'We're all ready to ride now, I reckon,' he said calmly.

'Good.' Dan nodded. He touched spurs to his mount, rode beside the other out of the homestead, and they took the trail that wound up in dog-leg fashion over the narrow footbridge over the nearby stream, across the wide meadow which shone with an eerie light in the moonlight, striking out into the night darkness, past a small herd of cattle bedded down for the night and then on through timber, with not a single light anywhere and the aromatic smell of the pines in their nostrils, sweet and heavy. The underbrush was a matting of pine needles, falling over the years to form a thick carpet that muffled all sound. The trail dropped on into a narrow draw, then climbed up the other side, going up the bare side of a hill. It took another three hours hard riding before they finally spotted the Trace below them. Dan reckoned they had hit it some ten miles or so west of New Orleans coming overland by this route, but it would soon be dawn and riding in broad daylight presented a problem to them.

The same thought had obviously occurred to Callard, for he reined his mount and inclined his head in the direction of the Trace. 'We don't have enough men with us to take them on even terms. We'll have to rely on surprise and in daylight that isn't going to be easy.'

'You reckon we ought to rest up until night?'

Callard debated that. 'It would be the wisest thing to do,' he said finally. 'I know what's in your mind, my friend. But somehow, I doubt if Tollinson will harm the girl so long as he figures there's a chance you might give yourself up. I think Thorpe is telling the truth there. Another few hours will make little odds to the outcome of this.'

Dan tightened his lips. The thought of the girl in the the hands of those outlaws, not knowing what was going to happen to her, or what was happening outside, whether anyone knew what had occurred, or whether there was anything being done to help her, almost broke him in half. But he forced himself to think clearly, to look at this rationally. If they rushed in, they could end up by all being destroyed and that would help no one. He forced patience into his mind, nodded in agreement.

A mile further on, they crossed a river born high in the hills, the clear water tumbling over the rocky bed as it rushed down the side of the hill out on to the plain below. There was, Dan considered, little chance of them being spotted here by anyone on the Trace. They fought their way over some of the roughest ground Dan had ever encountered, came to where a wide chute of loose earth ran down for perhaps a quarter of a mile, put their horses to it, the animals slithering down stiff-legged as they fought to retain their balance, their riders leaning hard back in the saddles. In places, only Dan's added weight on the saddle prevented the horse from slipping all the way down the steep slope. This was the way of it for twenty minutes while the dawn brightened greyly in the east and the moon dimmed appreciably along the other horizon. At the bottom of the wrinkle of rock, they hit a narrow Indian trail that led up into clumps of pine and sage and made better time here, giving their mounts their heads. Evidently Callard knew where he was going, had probably travelled this trail many times in the past, for he led the way obviously unconcerned. Turning a sharp corner where tall boulders, higher than a man lifted sheer on either side, they came into a rocky clearing, with trees growing at intervals about it, providing them with some kind of cover. There were the remains of a fire in the middle of the clearing, with a circle of loose rocks piled around it.

The men dismounted, left their horses in a loose bunch at the edge of the clearing where the rocky walls were highest. Here, there was little chance of them straying.

A fire was lit and soon there was a can of hot coffee hanging over it, bubbling in the growing sunlight, the appetising aroma filling the air.

Callard sat on a low rock beside Dan, pointed along the narrow canyon that opened out on the other side of the clearing, dipping down steeply to the Trace.

'From here, we can catch any sound at all down there. The canyon acts as a natural funnel.' He gave the surrounding terrain a keen survey in the growing daylight. Dan sat back to roll a cigarette. He relished the smoke after the long night ride and drank the coffee which one of the men brought him slowly, feeling it add its own brand of warmth and energy to his body. Sunlight began to move over the hills, wave upon wave of yellow light, touching first the crests and then flowing down the steep sides, leaving only the deeper chasms in full shadow.

'This place begins to get hot during the morning,' observed Callard. 'I used to come here often. A good place from which to keep an eye on the Trace.' He lit a cigarette. 'Used to be that a man had to keep a close watch. Outlaws were ready to burn any man's place down. Now we know who our enemies are.'

After he had eaten, Dan dropped on his shoulders, pulled his broad-brimmed hat down over his eyes, grateful for the rest, forcing himself not to think of why he was here, knowing that there was nothing he could do about it during the day. He was grateful for the chance to be able to do a little clear thinking, his thoughts uncluttered by the necessity for urgent action. All he wished was a straight chance at Tollinson and Vannier, an even encounter. He wanted nothing more, except perhaps to know that the girl was safe. He felt a tinge of envy as he thought vaguely of Aaron Lewis. Even though he had been badly hurt, he did not doubt that the lawyer would pull through all right with the doctor keeping an eye on him, and with a girl like Jennifer King to marry, Lewis was a man who seemed to have everything to live for. And as for himself, what would be left for him to do when all this was over, assuming he came out of it with a whole skin? Would he continue to ride the never-ending trail which seemed to lead to nowhere? At the moment he could see nothing else open to him. He turned a little on the hard ground, aware of the movement of men and horses all about him in the growing heat of the flooding sunlight. The thought had brought the old, familiar ache back into his mind again, the feeling that life would be nothing more than an endless succession of nights and days as far as he was concerned, a round of riding and staying here and there along the trails, not remaining in the one place for any length of time, always with that restlessness bubbling up in him, dogging his heels.

Bitterness came up in him for a moment, welling into his mouth and he could taste it on his tongue. So long as there were men like Tollinson around, he knew he would continue to fight the world and its evils. He felt his fists clench tightly by his sides, forced himself to relax. The food he had eaten acted as a sopofiric and he fell asleep, his body surrendering to the fatigue that existed in his bones and limbs.

When he woke, the sun was already past its zenith and beginning to dip to the west, throwing shadows over the clearing from the opposite direction. The trees stirred a little in the breeze which had blown up, leaves rustling on the branches.

Callard came off the rock into sight. He squatted on his heels, nodding his head slowly. 'We spotted a couple of riders a long way off to the west,' he said conversationally. 'They kicked up a lot of dust which enabled us to see them, but they just seemed to be riding around, probably a couple of Tollinson's men watching the trail. I figure he's hidden out in that direction, there are plenty of rocks there and he could be in one of the caves there, well away from the Trace.'

Callard dropped on one elbow, content with the day. 'I'm wondering how far we can trust Thorpe,' he said after a brief, reflective pause.

'You reckon he'll try to double-cross us and warn Tollinson?'

'Well, it will be the only way he can get back into Tollinson's good books after the way he bungled his mission last night.'

'Could be,' Dan agreed. He did not like the idea of those two men who were probably watching the trail. It seemed to him that Thorpe was more likely to try to warn them in some way. Then they would do the rest, heading back to where Tollinson and the rest of his men were. Once the element of surprise was lost, they would have a fight on their hands which might prove too much for them. He did not know, as yet, how the men who were riding with them would fight when it came to the inevitable showdown. Could they be trusted to stand their ground, in the face of men such as Tollinson had riding with him, professional killers, wanted by the law in perhaps half a dozen states? It was a question which could only be answered, one way or the other, when the time came, but until then it would always pose a question mark in his mind.

He shrugged and sat up, stretching his limbs. The hot sun had burned his face in spite of the hat he had drawn over his eyes and he touched his flesh gingerly with the tips of his fingers. A quick squint at the sun told him that it still wanted several hours to sundown and they would not be able to ride out much before then. Once they left this clearing and took the narrow canyon down to the Trace, they ran the risk of being spotted by any look-outs Tollinson may have planted along the main trail.

They made another meal, ate it in silence, Thorpe accepting his share with a sullen lack of grace. His forehead was deeply furrowed and he seemed to be thinking deeply, probably trying to figure out a way out of this mess. There was a distinct look of fear at the back of his eyes. He had lived too long with violence not to be afraid now.

The afternoon passed slowly but the heat had increased in its suffocating, piled-up intensity, giving them little respite from it. Dan felt the edge of heat making him more nervous and jumpy than he liked and it was difficult for him to concentrate. He tried to plan ahead, to work out the best way to take Tollinson by surprise. First of all, they would have to take care of any men watching the trail, and take them silently. When that was done, everything would rely on forcing Thorpe to lead them to the right place and not into a trap. He vowed then that Thorpe would get the first bullet if he did try to double-cross them. He had come through too much to be cheated of a chance at Tollinson and Vannier now.

At six o'clock, the sun dipped more swiftly towards the hills to the west, and the shadows grew long and dark over the country with the yellow dust streak of the Trace clearly visible where it ran almost due west towards the setting sun. The sky turned red and yellow at the same time with the blueness deepening to the east as night moved in.

After the sun dropped out of sight in a blaze of crimson, the world changed, became blue and cool with only a slight residual heat still clinging to the air. There was the sharp smell of the hills now, flowing like wine over the trail. The last of the coffee was drunk and the fire kicked out. The horses were saddled up and the men prepared to ride out, checking their guns with a nervous unease.

Dan walked over to where Thorpe stood beside his mount. He said softly and distinctly. 'If you've got any ideas in your mind about giving us away to Tollinson once we hit the Trace, Thorpe, I'd forget 'em right now. Because I'll kill you the minute you make a wrong move. Get that?'

Thorpe licked his lips dryly, nervously, then nodded, his Adam's apple bobbing up and down in his neck.

# 7

## Settler Law

They stayed with the main trail upward and it took them presently to a long stretch of timber, beyond which lay the canebrake and then the rocky slopes where Thorpe maintained they would find Tollinson. Once near the timber, they wheeled aside from the trail and halted their mounts out of sight of anyone who might be watching from higher up near the canebrake.

Dan slid from his saddle, checked his guns, then said tersely to Callard, 'I'm going to take care of the man who's watching the trail. We'll have to make sure of him before it's safe to go on.'

The settler nodded in agreement, made to swing down. 'You may need help,' he said harshly. 'I'll come with you.'

'No.' Dan shook his head. 'One man might get close enough where two would be spotted.' There was a hard touch of menace in his tone as he added. 'This shouldn't take too long. Keep an eye on Thorpe while I'm gone. I wouldn't like to think that he may be close behind me.'

Callard hesitated with some reply forming in his mind. Then he nodded, lips clamped tight. 'He won't give us any trouble,' he said grimly.

Sheltered by the trees, Dan moved noiselessly through the thick timber. He did not dare stick to the Trace at this point, not knowing where the look-out might be situated, and he found that he could move faster through the brush on foot than he would have been able to do on horseback. Reaching the far edge of the timber, he crouched down for a moment and watched the open area over which he would have to move to reach the canebrake. The trail swung away to the left of his position and he could just see it, where it ran on into the thick cane. There was a small rocky outcrop less than fifty yards away, overlooking this stretch of the Trace and it came to him that this was probably the best place for a man to lie in wait for anyone happening along the Trace. In the dimness, he could make out little beyond the rough outline of the rocks. For all he knew, a man could be there at that very moment, eyes alert, watchful for the first sign of trouble. Once he picked out the sound of riders in the distance, he would double back to warn Tollinson. He knew he would have to work his way closer before he could be sure.

He debated the position for a long moment, then knew that there was nothing for it but to move out into the open and trust to his luck that the man, if he was there, would be keeping an eye on the Trace and not watching the terrain at his side. Slithering forward, keeping his head well down, he wormed his way over the rough ground, making no sound at all. This was work he knew well, a man in his element, moving as soundlessly as any Indian.

The man was seated on a flat section of rock with his back to him, smoking a cigarette. It was the scent of cigarette smoke on the faint breeze which had alerted Dan to the other's presence long before he could see his vague shadow. There was a rifle propped against the rock beside him, within easy reach of his hand, but the other seemed to be completely relaxed as though expecting no trouble, confident that the nearest enemy was many miles away. If Tollinson was sharing this sort of optimism, it ought not to be too difficult to take him by surprise, reflected Dan as he eased his way closer, pulling himself forward with his hands.

The sound of a rider came out of the stillness behind him. Cautiously, Dan flattened himself to the ground. He was now so close to the look-out that he could almost have reached out and touched the man. The rider came out of the night and halted his mount a couple of yards away in the middle of the trail.

'Anything happening, Ben?' he called softly.

The man on the rock eased himself to his feet, shook his head. 'Nothing so far,' he replied. 'You reckon he'll come?'

There was a note of grim certainty in the other man's tone as he answered: 'He'll come all right, make no mistake about that. If he doesn't come tonight, then it'll be tomorrow, or the day after. But he'll come.'

'You figure that lawyer fella is dead?'

A pause, then the other muttered harshly, with a faint laugh. 'Reckon he must be. I don't usually miss, especially at that range.'

'If he ain't, and Carson manages to get to him in time, he could tell him a whole lot about our hideout.' The other eased himself forward in the saddle with a creak of leather. 'Even if that's the case, I figure Carson will still come riding out when he hears about the girl.'

'She giving any more trouble?'

'None so far. I reckon she's resigned herself to the fact that she won't be able to get away.'

Dan let his breath go in slow, easy pinches through his nostrils at the other's words. At least, Jennifer was still alive. For a while, he had been plagued by the feeling that maybe she had been killed after all and Tollinson had been merely using this as bait to draw him into the trap which had evidently been laid for him. The other's words had also told him that they were evidently not expecting him to have any men to back him up when he did come. That meant they were pretty certain Thorpe had carried out the task which had been allotted to him and had finished the settlers once and for all. There was a faint feeling of grim amusement in his mind as he lay there, face pressed into the cold rock, holding himself absolutely still. The men talked for a little while, then the man on horseback wheeled his mount and rode back along the Trace, the steady beat of his mount fading into the distance until it was gone altogether. The look-out lowered himself back on to the rock, tossed the butt of his cigarette away and stared off towards the east.

Rising silently from the rocks at the back of the man, Dan was on him before he knew he was there. The man half turned as if some hidden instinct warned him of danger, then the butt of the revolver smashed hard against the back of his head, pitching him forward with only a faint moan escaping from his lips. He hit the rocks and lay still.

Easing the other into the rocks, Dan bent and felt for the pulse. It still beat faintly against the man's wrist. Dragging him where he would not be seen by anyone riding the Trace, he went back to rejoin the others waiting in the timber.

'It's done,' he said shortly. 'There was another man came up from the rear. They've got the girl somewhere close by.'

'This other man,' said Callard. 'What did you do with him?'

'Let him ride back before knocking out the look-out. If he hadn't got back to Tollinson, they would have become suspicious. I figure nobody will bother riding out to check again for some hours. By that time, we should have found them and finished what we have to do.'

Thorpe said: 'Now that you're here you won't need me to continue the ride with you. I could stick back here. I've kept my part of the bargain and — '

Dan shook his head. 'You ride on with us, Marshal,' he said thinly, in a tone which brooked no argument. 'If there are any bullets flying, you'll be right up there with us, so I figure it will be to your advantage not to try any tricks.'

Thorpe licked his lips, then moved up with them as they rode out through the first-growth timber, cutting along towards the open ground. They rode past the upthrusting rocks where the look-out had been, then on into the cane, moving slowly, not wanting the sound to carry in the night stillness which pressed down like the flat of a hand all around them, hemming them in. Once well inside the cane, Dan reined up, motioned Thorpe forward.

'I can smell wood smoke,' he said softly, keeping his voice down. 'Is this the place?'

'Yes, About four hundred yards that way, up the rock face. There's a narrow trail leading up to it, cutting away from the cane about fifty yards further on.'

Dan nodded. He knew instinctively that the other was telling the truth. As far as Thorpe was concerned, the time for dying was past. Speaking to the men, Dan said: 'We dismount here and go the rest of the way on foot. Better tether your horses so they won't stray.'

He waited until the men had swung down from the saddle, moving their mounts to the far side of the trail, tethering them to the stout cane. Callard came up, nodded his head lowly, sniffing at the air. 'They got themselves a fire built,' he observed. 'Maybe they are only expecting you to show up.'

'That's what I'm gambling on. Get your men and spread them out on either side of that trail which cuts up into the rocks, then move up slow and quiet, and spread out at the top. I want Tollinson to think he's only got me to contend with before we all move in.'

'Why don't we just rush him, hem him inside the cave and cut down any man who pokes his nose outside?' murmured one of the men.

'Because he could get the girl while we're doing that. Even if we were to attack in force, she would still be in danger. No, we have to try to get her out before we attack.'

'You thinking of going in there alone?' Callard looked at him with a curiously bright glitter in his eyes. 'You'd never have a chance. He'll have more men in that cave than we have out here.'

'That's a risk I have to take,' said Dan grimly. He checked his guns, filled a couple of empty chambers from his belt, then moved forward. 'Wait for my signal,' he said tersely. 'Then move in.'

Callard nodded, his face serious. He gestured towards his men and they began to scatter, slipping away through the tall cane in the direction of the rocks. Dan paused for a moment to peer about him in the darkness. The range of low hills formed a darker smudge on the skyline where they lifted towards the star-strewn heavens. As he moved swiftly in front of the others, leading the way towards the incline, Dan wondered what he might find up there. Was Tollinson really so confident that he could not be taken by surprise and in force, that he had left only that one man to watch the trail from New Orleans — with maybe another look-out watching in the other direction?

Success seemed to be dependent on so many imponderables and there was a riot of half-formed thoughts and ideas racing in turmoil through his brain as he reached the bottom of the steep slope, crouching down among the last of the cane where it dribbled out into open ground. Straining his ears to pick out any sound from the rocks above him, he tried to estimate where the outlaws were holed up, but there was only the faint murmur of the breeze in the handful of stunted trees and bushes that grew alongside the rocky ledges.

Finally, he was satisfied and edged his way forward, crawling on hands and knees over the rough rocks, moving with the quiet stealth of an Indian. A dark shadow, he slipped from one concealing patch of darkness to another. It was just possible that there might be another man keeping watch outside the cave and a moment later, he spotted the other a few yards away to his left. He drew in a sharp breath. The man had turned his head and seemed to be staring right at him, his face shadowed. It seemed incredible that the other did not see him, lying there, but the man made no move, and gradually Dan let the breath ease out through his tight lips. His hand closed around one of the guns, easing it from its holster. Reversing it, he gripped the barrel tightly in his fingers, padded on silent feet towards the mesquite just behind the guard, was on top of the other before the man was even aware of the presence of danger. Swiftly, he brought the butt of the gun down with a sickening thud on top of the man's head, caught him by the shoulders as he slumped forward, lowering the unconscious body into the rocks without a sound. Less than ten seconds later, he was moving quickly towards the wall of rock where he reckoned the cave to be and there had not been a single sound to indicate that the outlaws had heard anything.

This was going to be the tricky part. He could smell the wood smoke more keenly now, passed another clump of thorn, ignoring the scratches on his hands and knees. Bending, he scanned the coarse-grained rock, moving his gaze slowly along it, striving to pick out any change in the colour or texture. It took him several seconds to make out where the tarp had been hung over the cave entrance. The outlaws had been clever, had not intended that the cave should be seen from the Trace. Most other men would have stared at the tarp without even seeing it.

Softly, he moved towards it, glanced up and noticed the narrow ledge that ran along the top of the cave, possibly three feet above it. The ledge came down about ten yards further on. By now his eyes were accustomed to the blackness of the moonless night. The bright starlight laid a faint, shimmering glow and within seconds, he was edging along the ledge, crouching down within inches of the cave. Now that he was so close, it was possible to pick out the voices of the men inside the cave. He clearly heard Tollinson's harsh voice and on one occasion, another man spoke up and he had the unshakeable impression that it was Vannier. So the outlaw leader from Natchez-under-the-Hill had come to be in at the kill. A sense of grim amusement ran through Dan as he gripped his weapons tightly. Reaching out with one foot, he tipped a large stone over the side of the ledge, heard it crash on to the ground immediately outside the cave entrance and go bounding off down the slope. The racket sounded deafening in the taut silence. There was a moment of quietness inside the cave and then Tollinson's harsh voice yelling orders. Down below Dan, the tarp was twitched aside and a small bunch of men stepped out cautiously, peering about them into the darkness.

'That you, Ben?' Tollinson's voice sounded in a tight yell. When there was no answer, the outlaw said: 'That's damned funny. Henshaw, take a couple of men with you and check those trees yonder. It's just possible Carson might have slipped past Ben. If he's there, take him alive. I want to see him die and know who pulled the trigger.'

Three men moved off over the rough, stony ground. Dan let them get a few yards away, then lowered his guns on to Tollinson's back and said thinly: 'Hold it right there, Tollinson, or I'll shoot you in the back as you deserve.'

He saw the man stiffen, hands hovering just above his gunbelt. Then the other whirled, yelled loud and long, threw himself down and tried to roll away, expecting a bullet in his back at any moment. The rest of the men with him scattered and at that same moment, with a suddenness that was startling, even though Dan had been expecting it, the silence of the night around the cave erupted with gunfire. The brief stabbing flashes of orange light from the barrels of the guns were from the direction of the trees all around the wide clearing in front of the cave.

With a savage, bitter oath, Tollinson fired up at the ledge where Dan lay hidden.

'Get the girl,' he yelled. 'We'll kill her, Carson, if you don't call off your men.'

Lead fanned Dan's cheek as he moved forward. This was what he had anticipated, but now he had Tollinson and most of his men outside the cave, lying on the ground as they sought to take cover from the flailing lead that hummed viciously through the air over their heads, pinning them down. There was no point in maintaining silence now that their presence had been discovered. Quickly, he reached the edge of the ledge, dropped into space. He hit the ground hard, rolled over once or twice, came on to his feet like a cat, the guns in his hands spitting lead at the men around him. He heard one man yell with the pain of a smashed shoulder. Then he was racing for the cave entrance, pulling the tarp aside.

He heard the girl scream as he ran in. A quick glance showed him the square form of Vannier moving quickly to the rear of the cave where the girl lay on an outcrop of rock, arms and legs bound. There was a deep and burning anger inside Dan as he ran forward, feet slipping on the treacherous floor of the cave. The flickering light of the fire showed him that there were other men there. His sudden appearance had taken them all by surprise.

Bullets whistled about him as he dived for cover to one side, aiming a quick shot at Vannier. He caught the gleam of the knife in the outlaw's hand as the other moved in on the girl. Dan's first shot took the man in the shoulder, the leaden impact whirling him round on his feet, bringing him face to face with Dan. Triggering swiftly, he loosed off another couple of shots, saw Vannier lift up on to his tiptoes, take three half-running steps backward, hands clawing in front of him. Then he dropped, head striking the rock wall of the cave at his back. The life went out of his eyes, but Dan scarcely noticed. Without pausing to think, oblivious of his own safety, he ran towards the girl, grabbed her with one arm and pulled her down behind the rocks. A slug whined off the rock within inches of his head, screeching into the back of the cave where it ricocheted again as it struck another unyielding surface obliquely.

More gunfire deafened him as he lay there. He gave the girl a quick glance, forcing a smile. Her answering smile was a little wan, but there seemed little fear in her eyes.

For the moment, they were safe from the bullets, but it would only be a matter of time before the outlaws began to move in on them from two sides, working their way around the cave walls. Reaching into the pocket of his jacket, he pulled the knife out, sawed swiftly at the ropes which held the girl. They gave slowly, and several times he was forced to pause in his work and aim a snap shot at the men crouched near the cave entrance, firing across the fire at them, forcing them to keep their heads down.

At last, the girl was free and she lay behind the rocks, rubbing her wrists and ankles, striving to bring the circulation back into her chafed limbs.

'Are you all right, Jennifer?' he asked solicitously.

She gave a quick nod. 'How did you find me?' she asked breathlessly.

'I found Aaron Lewis on the trail a couple of days ago. He'd been shot in the back but I got him to New Orleans in time. He'll be all right in a few weeks, just lost a little too much blood, that's all.' He watched the change in her expression and saw a look of relief there, but little else.

'It takes all kinds to make a world,' Dan said. He risked a quick look around the rocks in front of him, saw three men edging their way forward on the far side of the cave. There was the sudden bark of a gun from the other side and the bullet screeched off the rock, sending fragments of stone into his eyes. He ducked sharply, then brought his head up again, fired swiftly at the crouching men, thumbing back the triggers of the guns. The echoes were thrown back at him from the walls of the cave. One of the outlaws yelled harshly, stumbled to his knees and pitched forward on to his face, the guns falling from his nerveless fingers. The other two hesitated, tried to run for cover and died a second later before they had taken a couple of paces back.

There was still the harsh, vicious rattle of gunfire outside the cave where Callard and the other settlers were pouring a steady stream of fire into the men who had rushed outside with Tollinson. Out of the corner of his eye, Dan saw the tarp that had been stretched in front of the entrance, shudder and jerk like a live thing as lead thudded into it.

Not trying to get up, realizing that with the men near the entrance of the cave watching for every move he made he would never make it, Dan lay beside the girl, thumbing the triggers back as fast as they would go. One man suddenly reared up from the shadow of the rocks, arms flailing high over his head as if trying to clutch at something high over his head. There was a look of stupefied amazement on his scowling features as his head snapped forward and he went down.

Inside the cave there was silence now. Dan lay perfectly still, listening to his heart thudding so violently against his ribs that he felt certain any of the outlaws still alive must be able to hear it. Nothing seemed to move in the darkness that lay beyond the orange circle of firelight.

'Stay here,' he whispered to the girl. 'There may be some of them still alive here.'

Cautiously, he felt his way forward, one six-gun in its holster, the other balanced in his right hand. His finger was hard on the trigger and every nerve in his body was screaming with the rising tension, every muscle tight with anticipation. Strangely now, there was none of the exhilaration he usually felt at a time like this, stalking killers who would shoot him in the back without warning if they were given half a chance. Instead his mind felt empty and dull and there was the growing feeling that things had happened too easily, were going too well for them. Tollinson would not be standing still while this attack was going on.

There was a faint sigh somewhere to his right. He paused instantly, freezing as he tried to locate the sound. It had been a sudden gasp for air which had given away the presence of someone still alive, and close on its heels there had been the faint scrape of metal against rock as if a man had moved uneasily, not liking the growing stillness, and his revolver had caught on some out-thrusting spur of rock. Very slowly, Dan turned his head, trying to make out where the man lay hidden. His shoulder blades began to itch intolerably and he expected a bullet to come from the shadows at any moment, slamming into his body, cutting through flesh and bone.

He could just make out the heap of tumbled rocks on one side of the cave entrance and his lips curled into a tight grin. That was the most obvious place for a man to hide if he intended to shoot down anyone moving forward from the rear of the cave. He was debating in his mind whether to creep forward a little further and force the other out into the open, when there came a sudden hard volley of fire from immediately outside the cave. Silence followed close on the heels of the racket and then Callard's voice, just beyond the tarp, called loudly:

'You in there, Carson?'

The other's words echoed briefly around the cave and were then drowned by the thunderous explosion of a single gunshot. Dan whirled, lips drawn back in a vicious snarl. That shot had come, not from the pile of rock where he had considered the outlaw to lie hidden, but from the other side of the cave. The sharp stab of orange flame caught his attention immediately. He knew with a sudden certainty that had it not been for Callard calling out like that, he would have been shot down without warning the second he slithered out into the open. Whirling savagely, feeling the anger grow in him, he edged to his left, dived for the rocks there, heard a slug bounce off the floor of the cavern at his heels. Then he was crouched under cover again and he lay quite still, waiting. These were the men who rode with Tollinson, he thought, feeling the hatred wash through him, the sort of men who had killed Nathan King, Jennifer's father, in cold blood, simply because he had dared to print the truth. The anger and the hatred made rock out of him and he knew he could lie there, utterly still, for as long as was necessary.

The man did not have the guts of many men he had known. A faint sigh came out of the other as the silence grew long. It was the sudden need for air, for movement of some kind which had betrayed the other and the man seemed to know it, for he suddenly began to fire with a desperate recklessness, sending bullets in every direction where he judged Dan to be. Dan counted four shots, heard them ricochet off the floor of the cavern and go screaming into the firelit darkness.

Reaching out, Dan felt for a rock, lifted it and tossed it high into the air so that it crashed to the ground some distance away. It drew a fifth shot from the other.

'You wasted that one,' he called thinly. 'I'm not there.' Ducking back, he waited for the last shot. When it did not come, he knew that the other was refusing to be drawn into wasting his ammunition. The man must have recognized the precariousness of his position now. He heard the soft scrape of the outlaw's body on the rock, then edged his way between a couple of tall boulders, peering round them. He could not see the man, but the other's shadow was clearly visible on the rocks.

Dan laid his gun on the clear patch and waited. He did not have long to wait. The other was short on pure nerve when it came to a situation like this. Therefore he wasn't surprised when he saw the shadow lift. The man was getting his legs under him, ready for a dash for the entrance of the cave, hoping to get out before Dan could get a killing shot at him. Drawing back his lips, he waited, finger hard on the trigger. The man suddenly loosed off another shot, then lurched to his feet and began to run. He was almost at the entrance when Dan shot him down. The man ran on as if unable to stop, then his legs slid from under him and he finished up on his face, his outstretched fingers just touching the tarp, now torn and shredded by the flailing bullets.

For a moment, Dan lay there, sucking air down into his lungs. Then he got slowly to his feet, walked over to the rear of the cave where the girl still lay behind the rocks. 'I reckon it's all over,' he said quietly. He thrust the guns back into their holsters. He heard men's voices outside and moved towards the entrance, the girl close behind him, stepping over the bodies of the men near the tarp.

Callard stood just beyond the opening, one arm hanging limply by his side. He threw the girl a quick, appraising glance, then looked directly at Dan. 'I figure we won't have any more trouble from these men,' he said simply. 'We got most of them. A bare handful rode over the hill. I reckon they'll just keep on riding until they get to the other side of the mountains. They won't come back this way, not with Tollinson gone.'

'Is he dead?' Dan asked pointedly.

The other nodded, led the way to a shallow depression in the rocks. The rancher lay on his back, sprawled among the boulders, arms flung out, dust on his face and hair where his hat had fallen off. In the first rays of the rising moon, Dan saw the look of amazement on the man's face, the eyes wide and staring. The thought of defeat had never entered the other's head. He had evidently been so supremely confident that he had everything under control, that he would have only one man to contend with.

Dan tapered up a cigarette, glanced about him at the grim-faced men who stood around in small groups. Now that the showdown was over, there was time to relax and think a little. Certainly with Tollinson and Vannier dead, and the gang either killed or scattered, there would be no further trouble here for the settlers. They would be able to live their lives in peace and it seemed unlikely that any other man like Tollinson would be able to ride into this territory and set himself up as the other had done. Perhaps now, the Government too would see to it that law and order was made and kept here. Slowly, the days of violence were dying. As the frontier was pushed further west across the vast stretches of the continent, a new race of men would come to take the place of the outlaws and killers who still, in places, roamed the Trace.

It was only a momentary thought. He turned to Callard. 'How's the arm?' he asked.

'Just a scratch,' said the other. He glanced down at the stain on the sleeve of his shirt. 'It'll wait until we get back to New Orleans.'

'Where's Thorpe?' Dan looked about him, then spotted the figure of the marshal a few yards away. He went over to the other, seeing the man's face, slack and open, in the growing moonlight.

'It's finished, Thorpe,' he said sharply. 'Tollinson and Vannier are dead. I reckon when we get back to town, we'll have to decide what to do with you. I know that if the settlers get their hands on you, they'll probably lynch you without a trial and it won't be any more than you deserve.'

'You wouldn't let them do that,' said the other sharply. He licked his lips and then rubbed the back of his hand over his mouth. 'I kept my side of the bargain. I brought you here like you said and you've got what you came for.'

Dan nodded. 'Somehow, I reckon you're not worth bothering about, Thorpe,' he said thinly, through his teeth. 'A man who wears a marshal's badge and throws in his lot with outlaws like those is less than a man.'

'They forced me to do it,' whimpered the other. 'I wanted no part of it, but it was their votes and money that put me into office and once they started, there was nothing I could do about it. They'd have killed me if I'd refused to do as they said and there would have been another man in my place, probably even worse than I was.'

Thorpe got no answer to that. Dan turned on his heel and walked back along the stony path to where the girl stood, looking up into the moonlight which flooded everything with its pale cold light. She did not seem to hear him coming, for she did not turn until he had come right up to her. He put his hand on her arm and saw her eyes widen a little as she turned her head. They were soft grey and there was a deeply luminous glow in them which he had not noticed before. He tried to tell himself that it might be something more than just a trick of the moonlight.

She drew in a short, swift breath. 'What will you be doing now that this is finished, Dan?' she asked in a low soft voice. 'You only came here to get even with Tollinson, and then with Vannier. Now that you've done it, I suppose you'll be riding out, heading over the hill after those other men who rode out a little while ago when the fighting got too tough for them.'

She watched him with a greater and greater closeness, watching as the hard solidness came to his face.

'I know that you think there's still something between Aaron and me. Maybe there was once, but no longer. He's a good man, a man of principles, but he prefers to let other people do the fighting to uphold those principles. I need a man who can tame me, who can fight for what he believes to be right. I don't ask that he should tell me his past, what happened before he came here. All I ask is that he should be a man and — '

'I suppose that it always gives a man a strange feeling to ride to the very end of one trail and not be able to discover the start of another.'

'There's one that could start right here, in New Orleans,' she said gently. 'We need a man who would stand up for everyone, not just the ranchers and cattlemen, but the settlers too, an impartial man who owes allegiance to no one but himself.'

'Are you saying that I ought to take Thorpe's place as marshal?'

'Yes.' He saw her face lift a little. 'But you must find your own wishes. I can't tell you what to do. This is a decision you have to make for yourself.'

'I wonder what Aaron would say to this?' he murmured, half to himself.

The girl caught the words. There was

a half smile on her lips, her eyes bright. 'It takes a long while and perhaps a lot of misery for anyone to really find themselves,' she said at last. 'I think that Aaron knows how I feel. It won't be much of a surprise to him.'

Dan nodded. He remembered some of the things that the lawyer had said that night after he had taken him to the doctor's after finding him on the trail. Even then, the other seemed to have realized that this might happen and Thorpe had suggested as much when he had claimed that it might have been Dan who had shot down the lawyer on the trail.

He thought about it and said softly: 'This is good country. There are sometimes men like Tollinson who set themselves up to destroy what is fine and good because of their own greed. I want to stay here. I want — ' He touched her with his arms. 'Is that the way it is with you?' he asked and tried to keep the wonderment out of his voice.

She nodded wordlessly. She did not move away at the increasing pressure of his fingers on her arms. She was smiling up at him, oblivious of the fact that Callard was standing only a few feet away, waiting for the men to come up from the trees.

Finally, the settler came over, said: 'I reckon there's nothing to keep us here now, Dan. Time we were moving out. There's a long trail to cover back to New Orleans.'

Dan nodded. There was a warm feeling inside him which he could not remember ever having experienced before. He had come to the end of one trail, a trail which had been filled with fear and violence; but as the girl had said, already there was a new one opening up ahead of him. As yet, he could only see a little way down it, but he had the unshakeable conviction that it would be a better trail to ride, that he would find there all that he had ever wished, the fulfilment of all the dreams he had ever had, sitting around a camp fire in the deep darkness and stillness of the night, watching the brilliant constellations wheeling across the sky from one horizon to the other, and wishing that he had someone to share all of this wonder with.

They moved off down the slope to the Trace, back to the trees where the horses were tethered, waiting for them. At the edge of the cane, the girl paused, threw one last glance over her shoulder in the direction of the low hills, now glinting greyly in the flooding moonlight. Dan felt the tension last for a few moments in her, then it was gone and she turned to walk beside him, her head held high.

## THE END